Praise

"Edgy, pacy, and chillingly real. A book you'll sink your teeth into and never forget."
JJ MARSH, AUTHOR OF *THE BEATRICE STUBBS SERIES*

"Few writers can bring rich, complex characters to life on the page in a way that Jessica Bell does. In *White Lady* she strikes at the heart of families in turmoil, giving a painfully honest portrayal of flawed humanity, while taking the reader on an intense, suspenseful ride rife with mystery. Be prepared to be wowed."
C. S. LAKIN, AUTHOR OF *INNOCENT LITTLE CRIMES*

"... this isn't for the faint of heart, but [Jessica Bell] does a fantastic job of giving real heart and motive to some really messed up people ... The character struggles weave together, clash and collide and as you can imagine, there is a lot of collateral damage ... if you like to see a bit of triumph in the wreckage, this may very well be for you."
HART JOHNSON, AUTHOR OF *A SHOT IN THE LIGHT*

about the author

Jessica Bell is an Australian award-winning author and poet, writing and publishing coach, and graphic designer who lives in Athens, Greece. In addition to her novels and poetry collections, and her best-selling *Writing in a Nutshell* series, she has published a variety of works online and in literary journals, including *Writer's Digest*.

Jessica is also the Co-Founder and Publisher of *Vine Leaves Press & Literary Journal*, a singer/songwriter/guitarist, a voice-over actor, and a freelance editor and writer for English Language Teaching publishers worldwide such as Macmillan Education and Education First.

Before she started writing she was just a young woman with a "useless" Bachelor of Arts degree and a waitressing job.

Visit Jessica's website: *jessicabellauthor.com*

Vine Leaves Press
Melbourne, Victoria, Australia

Second Edition
ISBN-13: 978-1-925417-50-0

First Edition published by Vine Leaves Press Australia, 2014.

Cover design by Jessica Bell
Interior design by Amie McCracken

National Library of Australia Cataloguing-in-Publication entry (pbk)
Creator: Bell, Jessica Carmen, author.
Title: White lady / Jessica Bell.
ISBN: 9781925417500 (paperback)
Subjects: Families--Fiction.
Organized crime--Fiction.
Suspense fiction, Australian.
Dewey Number: A823.4

white lady

jessica bell

Vine Leaves Press
Melbourne, Vic, Australia

"White covers a multitude of sins."
—Jonathan Milne

flash-forward

The road is cold and rough against my left cheek—the white reflection of the moon ripples in the pool of blood between me and Dad.

I blink, wince at a sharp pain in my thigh. I touch it with my right hand. It's wet, warm—a moist memory.

"Dad?" I whisper.

His eyelids flutter.

"Nash." I whisper a little louder, hoping he'll respond to his name instead. He remains still, silent, skeletal. I try to reach for him, but my left arm won't move. I'm not sure if I can even feel it.

Behind me, slow movement shifts the air. Someone curses under their breath and kicks a rock. It tumbles, rolls to a halt in the distance.

Gentle footsteps approach from behind. Someone sniffs, groans, and clears their throat; another voice whimpers.

A switchblade flicks open. The sound hovers in the air ...

chapter 1

mia

beer is not a protein drink

I pull my pyjama pants down with my eyes closed. If I open them, I'll get dizzy and panic. Touching the crevices that have formed from the tight elastic around my waist is enough to make me wanna puke.

"Don't look," I say to myself.

But I do.

I breathe through clenched teeth and shut my eyes so tight it makes them sting and water. I'm just getting bigger and bigger.

"Oh my god oh my god oh my god."

I grab my black tracksuit from my dresser drawer, the one with the writing on the arse that says *Lick Me*, and dress turned away from the mirror. I lower myself to the floor, lie on my stomach, and stare under my bed—the chocolate abyss. If I'm not careful it will suck me in. And once I'm in, I can't get out until I've eaten everything.

The key is to not even buy the chocolate, right? But I haven't got as far as that yet. But, you know, buying it isn't really the problem. Buying it doesn't mean I've gotta eat it. In fact, any time I like, I can chuck it away.

I can.

Really.

I reach under the bed and grab two family blocks of Cadbury's Double Decker chocolate. I unwrap them. Savouring the slow crackle of the tinfoil and ruffle of paper that makes the chocolate aroma wafting towards my nose an even better experience.

These blocks may be my last.

I put them on the floor between my spread legs. I stare at them. Squint at them.

"You are evil," I say to one block.

"You are eviler," I say to the other.

The female rockers plastered all over my walls glare at me with sexy smiles. Their poses are so hot and skin so glossy, I can imagine the sensation of Vaseline all over me.

I could have been one of them. I could have been a rock star.

Fat luck now. Ha! Get it?

"Resist," I say to myself. "Scribble down some lyrics to tame the beast."

But I don't.

I eat both blocks, staring at my hazy reflection in the glass cabinet door below the TV. For some reason I don't look as fat in that as I do in my mirror.

I polish off the chocolate—but I'm still hungry. Some bacon and eggs for breakfast would keep me good until lunch. I hope Dad hasn't thrown the bacon away after our "talk" last night.

"It's time to consider a serious diet," he said.

Am I ready for this?

My knees crack as I stand and turn to the mirror. I feel alright looking at myself when I'm dressed, when I've got my red lippy on and have a full stomach. I can pretend I'm pretty and sexy like my mum, that the boys at school still slip fuck-me notes into my locker, and that all the girls whisper in fear instead of making fun of me behind my back.

Thank God it's my last year of attending that hellhole.

I wink sarcastically at my reflection, run the tip of my tongue along my top lip.

And scoff at myself.

You fat cow.

One year ago, my reflection would have winked back at a flab-free fifty-four-kilo alabaster sex-bomb. At almost thirty kilos heavier, I'd be lucky if a rolling pin tried to have it on with me.

Seriously.

Runaway mother equals runaway diet and exercise regime. Runaway mother also equals beer and football with Dad in front of the box. Most weekends. Huh. Who am I kidding? *Every* weekend. Is it bad for me to say I enjoy that time with Dad a whole lot more than I ever enjoyed "quality" time with Mum shopping for the next best protein drink?

"I hate you," I say to myself in the mirror.

But I don't. I *despise* myself.

No positive thinking, or veggie diet, is gonna make me think better of myself. Sorry, Dad, but you're not the one with flabby armpits. Of course, you think it's all psycho-logical. It's not. It's physical. It's so physical that the hunger hurts. My stomach aches, my heart aches, my brain aches. This pain is real. I feel it. They're not just "stupid cravings that will subside with time."

What does he know?

He's never been fat.

I fill my schoolbag with the textbooks scattered all over my bed. I grab my open laptop by the screen, close it against my chest, and slide it into my schoolbag too. Maybe I'll find some dirt about the dickhead who stole my mother away. Botched surgeries. Hospital horror stories. You know the shit I'm talking about.

They always make me feel pretty.

And I *need* to feel pretty.

chapter 2

nash

yes. i smoke.

I reckon I change the channel every time Mia opens the fridge. It stops me wanting to glue the door to its frame. I can hear it in slow motion now: the extended pop of a suction pad to a smooth wet surface, sucking my daughter's face towards its fatty contents. The fridge door closes as fast as it opens, preceded by Mia's deep, raspy sigh.

I switch the channel one last time; lean over the coffee table; sip my double espresso; gather my packet of Drum, filters, papers to roll a few cigs. I sense Mia's laser-like stare from behind the kitchen counter as I stick the first rollie behind my ear. She wants me to let her off the hook. But I won't give in again. For the sake of her health, if anything. What kind of father would I be if I didn't put my foot down?

"Just try it, mate. One week. You won't feel so hungry."

I listen to the steadiness of my breath, watch as my calloused and bitten fingertips pinch tobacco into a neat line across the paper as though a different brain were giving my hands the orders. I roll the tobacco between my thumbs and forefingers, lick the edge of the paper, seal it into a perfect silky cylinder.

Wind howls and rattles the front door. Rain pelts down. For five seconds. Mia and I look at the ceiling with our mouths open. But then it just stops. Typical Melbourne weather.

I hold the cigarette in the air. A peace offering.

Mia drags her heavy feet across the carpet. A sound I associate with the Rottweiler we had when my ex-wife, Celeste, was still around. Before she discovered she could have the life she'd always dreamed of if she hooked up with that dirtbag plastic surgeon from LA, instead of roughing it out with a high school Phys Ed teacher with a fragile ego. I reckon what Celeste failed to realize was that it wasn't my fragile ego that screwed us up. We were doomed the day Celeste decided that my then-best mate, Ibrahim, was going to be the best man at our wedding.

Ibrahim.

All you need is to shake his hand and it's like signing away your life.

I hope he never comes back.

Mia snatches the cigarette out of my fingers and sits next to me. The leather couch sinks with a sigh. I turn to her, head still hanging, tilted to the side. She lights the cigarette with a match from her black polo shirt pocket. With only one drag, half of it disappears. I scrutinize Mia's puffy cheeks and the baby-like fat that's starting to form a double chin. I still think she's cute. But if she keeps going like this, I reckon I'll start seeing ugly.

My throat tightens at the thought, and I squint at her.

She's so beautiful inside and out. Why did Celeste push that health crap on her so much when she didn't even need it? She was fine. A normal healthy teenager who liked to eat chocolate now and again. She wasn't overweight. She was slim without even trying. Why did Celeste have to screw that up? Now Mia despises the thought of getting healthy so much that she doesn't understand the difference between trying to be healthy and obsessing over getting thin.

So what does she do? She eats.

She eats and eats and eats and eats. What *is* that? A "fuck you" to her mother? I reckon it is.

"Don't look at me like that." Mia blows smoke into my face and smirks.

"It's for your own good, mate." I lean forwards, run my tongue along my teeth, light my third rollie. I stare at the TV, elbows resting on my spread thighs, hands hanging between my knees.

Aussie Rules reruns.

If it weren't for Celeste and Mia, it would be someone else watching *me* kick the footy on the box. I internally shake the selfish thought from my head and wink at Mia.

She rolls her eyes, says, "Um. Hello? You're smoking?" and shoves me forwards. Ash falls onto the carpet. I spit on my finger and gently touch it. It sticks. I wipe it on the edge of my ashtray, the one Mia made me on her first day of high school. It looks like a pierced tongue, slightly cancerous.

Touché.

"I said, once you lose your first five kilos." I grab my red cap off the table and place it on my head, pulling the brim a little low over my eyes.

"It's too much. It'll take forever." Mia slouches.

"Then I'll quit in forever." I slap my hands on my knees and smile as though marking the conversation with a full stop.

Mia *tsks* and stands. Her knees crack, and her breath sounds thicker and heavier than usual. She walks to the kitchen, opens the fridge, flings her head backwards, and screams to the ceiling. "Fucking hell." She kicks the door shut. Bottles of beer rattle, and she starts to cry.

I butt out my cigarette and walk to the kitchen. Mia leans the top of her head against the fridge. Her shoulders shaking silently. This can't be easy for her. Can't be easy at all. And I honestly don't pretend to understand what it feels like. I've never had a weight problem. But I'll do what I can to support her through this. Ride the waves. I have to grit my teeth and be the mother for a while. What other choice do I have?

I pull her into my embrace from behind and kiss the top of her head.

"It's okay, mate." I whisper. "One day at a time."

But instead of responding the way I hope, with acceptance, with gratitude, Mia runs back to her bedroom in a fit of tears.

I give Mia half an hour to cool off before knocking on her bedroom door. I'm pleased she hasn't taken the collage of female rock legends off her door yet: Janis Joplin, Joan Jett, Suzie Quatro, lots I can't even remember the names of. Throw a female musician's name into a hat, and Mia probably wants to *be* her, no matter what generation they're from.

I reckon there has to be something in this to motivate Mia, to occupy her mind while she's on this diet. But no matter how many times I try to convince her to send her song lyrics to a magazine, she won't listen. She has no faith in herself. And I'm starting to sound like a broken record.

"Crikey, Mia, We gotta go. We'll be late." I lean in and knock again, my right cheek brushing against Debbie Harry's tit.

No answer.

I knock again.

Still no answer.

I open the door myself. She's not in there. And the place is spotless. Cleaning to avoid eating, maybe?

"Mia?" I call down the hallway. "You in the can?"

"Yeah." Her voice is muffled, annoyed.

"Hurry up. We gotta go."

"Yeah." This time followed by a cough.

I look at my feet, put my hands in my pockets. I hope she's not smuggling junk food into her bag again. I caught her doing that yesterday. She watched with tears in her eyes as I disposed of the cakes one by one. Looking back on that, I reckon it probably wasn't a good idea to rub her nose in it. But I wanted her to see how ridiculous it was. One cake? Fine. But *ten*?

"What you doin'?"

"Taking a shit. Need to know every fucking bowel movement?" The toilet seat clangs and water runs.

I scratch my beard. I take the pre-rolled cigarette from behind my ear, a Zippo out of my back jean pocket, light up, and lean my shoulder against the wall. Waiting.

Two full minutes later, Mia steps out of the bathroom. She sniffs and wipes her mouth on her shoulder. I squint with suspicion as I take the last drag.

"What?" Mia snaps, bringing her shoulders to her ears.

I flick my chin towards the front door. Mia adjusts the straps of her schoolbag and pulls her knickers out of her bum. I grab my keys and Drum off the coffee table as we pass it.

Mia puckers her brow. "You gonna teach PE in *jeans*?"

I hold the front door open and step to the side to let Mia out first. "Problem?"

Mia shrugs, heads towards our diarrhea-coloured Commodore, and mutters under her breath, "That's fucking pathetic."

I take one quick glance at the photo of me, Celeste, Ibrahim, and Sonia hanging on the wall—at our wedding before everything turned to shit—and think exactly the same thing.

chapter 3

mia
my epiphany

Before the bell rings for first period, I sit in the library with my laptop. I log on to the Internet and Google and type in "Dr. Karter Schwörer." He's the arsehole my mother tied the knot with. Ha! Tied the knot. Get it? Plastic surgeon . . . ? Okay, bad pun. Was never good at those anyway.

There are so many articles flaunting his breakthroughs in plastic surgery, but amongst them I find a list of Swiss surnames and their meanings. Out of curiosity, I scroll down to *Schwörer*.

"Nickname for 'conspirator in Swiss German.'"

I laugh and click back to the search bar.

Not exactly what I was after, but hey, it amused me for a moment. That's a positive step towards the Make Mia Feel Pretty Project.

It's so quiet in here. This library. I hate the quiet. When it's quiet, guilt creeps up on me. Guilt for eating too much. Guilt for being mean to Dad. But I can't help it. He pushes. Too hard. If he could just leave me be, to work this out for myself, then maybe I'd feel more confident that a diet is what I need. But right now, the diet feels forced on me. And useless. It's going to take forever for me to lose five kilos with what Dad wants me to do. Healthy balanced eating, my arse. There's gotta be an easier, faster way.

I scroll, scroll, scroll through the headlines in Google. Just one thing. One new picture of some deformed rich bitch to lift my spirits before class. But they're all the same. No new botched surgeries have been reported since yesterday morning.

Damn.

Just as the bell rings, I refresh the page one last time—you know, just in case—and spot an article entitled "Billionaire Karter Schwörer accused of falsifying data to push boy with deformed face to top of pro bono list." It's literally just gone up one minute ago.

Huh. Sorry, this doesn't make me feel pretty. It just makes me feel sick. Poor kid!

But wait . . . sick?

Oh man . . . why didn't I think of puking to get thin before?

chapter 9

nash

it's not just a simple touch

I slip into the staff room and sit at my desk without being noticed. Or, at least, I don't notice being noticed thanks to the brim of my cap—my psychological bodyguard. I switch on my computer, open the third drawer, and pull out a banana from my fruit stash. My high school footy mates, Gaz and Ibrahim, offer me a thumbs-up from the computer screen. I smile, nod, and chew—the good old days before Ibrahim got mixed up with the wrong crowd and almost destroyed my life.

I don't know why I still have pictures of him on here. I s'pose I'm not ready for our friendship to be as good as dead yet. I'd never have hooked up with Celeste if it wasn't for him. And if it wasn't for Celeste, I wouldn't have Mia.

I remember when me, Gaz, and Ibrahim would play footy, Celeste would gear up in blue and white and root for me like a true Aussie bloke. Face and hair all dolled up like Barbie, body like a tomboy just out of the sandpit. Tits totally flat. But I was never a tit man. I prefer a nice meaty arse to grab on to. My smile falls from my face at the thought of Celeste with Karter.

"Coffee?"

I look up mid-chew, at Sonia Shâd, the Advanced Mathematics teacher (okay, we're also doing it), who is handing me a dose of caffeine juice, the outside of my mug stained from overflow.

Sonia shrugs. "You know how it is."

I smile, nod, take the mug. It burns my hand, and I spill some on my jeans in my haste to put it on my desk.

"I am sorry," Sonia says. "I will get you a sponge."

"Nah, mate. Don't worry about it. Gotta change into my sports gear soon anyway."

Sonia smiles, tight-lipped. Folds her arms under her breasts, sways on the balls of her feet. We stare at each other while I sip my coffee. I slurp. Three times.

Her Goody Two-Shoes act creeps me out a bit. But it's good for her, I know this. I don't reckon I'd have as much willpower as she, given the situation. You really have to commend her efforts.

Sonia clears her throat. Does she want something? I glance at my computer screen as it shoots off e-mail notifications. Now my wallpaper flashes Celeste and Mia holding up that massive snapper for the camera. She's decked out in waterproof fishing pants, gumboots, hair scraggly from the wind, eyes squinting from the overcast glare at Sandy Point.

I reckon Mia was happy then.

Crikey. We were all happy.

"You are not doing too well, are you?" Sonia says, checking left and right as if to make sure no one's listening in.

"Nah. I'm fine." I look up. Sonia's eyebrows are practically touching her heart-shaped hairline. "Promise."

I pinch my nostrils with my forefinger and thumb to make sure there aren't any nose hairs sticking out. I swivel my seat to face the computer straight on, open my e-mail and a reply window to make myself look busy.

I can see Sonia in the corner of my eye, nodding a few too many times. She gently punches me on the shoulder.

"I am free after recess," she says.

"Yep. Me too."

I move a few papers around my desk and accidentally push the tip of my finger into a stray tack.

I curse under my breath and bring my finger to my mouth, but Sonia grabs my hand and stares at it. I let her watch as a drop of blood drips onto my desk before realizing what's going on and yank my hand away.

"Hey," I say with a frown.

Sonia's breath quivers as she deeply inhales. She blinks, coughs into her fist. "Right. See you after recess."

I smile and nod. She stumbles a little as she walks to her cubicle.

I stare at my screen, flexing my fists under the desk, hoping she's going to be okay. I reckon I should go over and give her a neck rub. But maybe I should also leave her alone. I'm never too sure whether my affection is a distraction or reminder, so I usually let her initiate it.

I decide to stay put.

I click my e-mail closed to reveal a shot of me and

Celeste as teenagers in our murky-green school uniforms. She's blowing cigarette smoke into my mouth, her feathery blonde hair teased high enough to nest squirrels, my fringe gelled into a wave.

It was three weeks before I decided to skip tryouts for the Carlton AFL team.

I remember because she told me she was pregnant.

And wasn't sure if it was mine.

chapter 5

mia

i deserve it

I reach my classroom in the new science wing, sweaty and flushed, ankles tight. The insides of my bum cheeks burn like someone has rubbed them with sandpaper. If only I could shove an ice pack between my legs, I'd feel a little more human and less like pork-spit-walking.

Everyone is seated, and Mrs. Shâd is writing the answers to yesterday's algebra homework on the board. I take a seat at the desk that's always left empty, as if sitting there might mean they'll catch my fat like a disease. I don't drop any books, and I make minimal noise. An achievement on most days.

The room is dead silent, bar the chalk that scrapes rather than slides across the blackboard. Before writing on the board, Mrs. Shâd used to dip the chalk in water. Not only were we spared the cringe-worthy squeaks and scratches but the symbols dried bright and bold, and you didn't have to squint if you were sitting at the back. But the principal told her it used the chalk too fast and therefore school funding.

What a tosser. He even checks in to make sure she's stopped doing it.

If there's one thing I've noticed since being transferred

to Mrs. Shâd's class, it's that she tries—even down to the simplest of things—to make school life glide rather than stutter. And I never used to appreciate how small acts of kindness made such a difference until I became this stinking ugly bitch-face and started paying more attention to others. Even if only because I can't stand my own existence.

I know. You're thinking, why was I transferred? Well, what do you think? The oblivious principal put me back into the class that is taught by Mr. Monroe. I couldn't stand him last year; I was certain he was dropping his pens by my desk so he could look up my skirt. So I kicked up a stink. Cried sexual harassment. He denied it, of course. But at least I got something positive out of it: Mrs. Shâd. She's cool.

Mrs. Shâd spins around, the sheen of her dark-grey pencil skirt catching the sunlight as she moves. She doesn't even have to smile. The kindness shining from her presence alone is enough to make me feel guilty for surfing the Net before class instead of finishing my homework.

Mrs. Shâd swivels around holding her chalk in the air. "I trust you have your answers ready to compare with those on the board." She looks straight at me as if she somehow knows I didn't finish.

As I yank my notebook from my bag, a tampon slips out from between its pages and rolls down the aisle. I snort as if the class has already broken out in laughter, and I have to join in to hide my humiliation.

Mrs. Shâd glides past, scoops the tampon up in a funnel of papers and drops it in my bag with a wink.

Just as I think the incident has gone unnoticed, a dude from the back row asks, "So how do ya decide where to stick those, Rebel?"

Cute. But I'm not as big as Rebel Wilson, thank you very much.

All heads turn to him. Some sneak glances at me. But my smirk slightly fades when I realize who made the remark. I swivel round in my seat and squint at him. At Mick. The dickhead who gets away with everything because he was diagnosed with ADD. The one that had an obsessive crush on me a year ago when I was still skinny, and I always turned down, then pashed his best friend in front of his face just to piss him off.

Yeah, I know. That wasn't a really smart move.

I would give anything to take that back now. To be skinny again, to kiss again, to actually accept Mick's offer and go out on that date without an ulterior motive. After all this time of hating body-builder muscles, his are starting to look attractive to me.

But. I deserve his shit. And won't fight it.

You know what? Bring it on.

Mrs. Shâd squeezes my shoulder. I flinch. No charity. Not now. It's pure bully bait. I know. I used to be Queen Bitch of Thornbury High. The one all the girls hated but still wanted to be. The one the boys wanted to fuck but wouldn't dare try. Hey, that rhymes. Mental note to jot it down in my lyric book.

Mick leans back, spreads his legs, picks a pimple. "I mean,

wouldn't it just get lost everywhere except your nostrils?" he says.

Some students giggle, others snicker, pens drop to desks, heads bow to chests. There goes that rhyming again.

"Mick," Mrs. Shâd snaps, now standing at the front of the classroom. "That is a terrible thing to say. Apologize."

It *was* a horrible thing to say, but I'm not gonna let it get to me. Words are words. And I've got something like five tubes of Wite-Out in my pencil case.

Mrs. Shâd sifts through some papers on her desk as if the whole incident were evolving to plan, or maybe she's just tired of his disobedience. He really loves to screw with people's heads. In fact, he can get pretty disgusting at times.

Mick narrows his eyes at Mrs. Shâd for a moment before focusing on me again. When he stands, his chair scrapes against the floor and echoes through the classroom.

"And to think I once wanted to stick my dick into your skanky cunt."

Student murmurs and giggles crawl the classroom walls like vines. Wow. That totally wasn't called for. Okay, maybe that hurt a bit. Maybe a bit more than a bit.

"Get out. Now!" Mrs. Shâd points towards the door, cheeks aflush.

Tears block my windpipe. But I can't let them out. Can't show it hurts.

Can. Not.

I glance at my bag. There are Lamingtons in there. I need them. To soak up all the self-loathing and mental vomit.

What's the point in trying to lose weight now, anyway? I'm too far fucking gone. I should just suck it up. Learn to live as if this were the way I've always been.

Mick drags his feet towards the exit.

And spits at me on the way by.

chapter 6

sonia

it was the back porch
that changed everything

It is mid-period, and the corridor is as silent as a morgue. I point my finger so close to Mick's forehead, I could engrave my initials into it with my nail. He has crossed the line one too many times. How much more do I have to "be sensible" and continue to watch him get worse and worse, more confidence shoved under his rebellious belt?

What now? Detention? Principal's office? Suspension? Again? All that's left is to expel him. But really? Does it have to come to that? *Should* it come to that? And I am so tired of the racism. Just because he is Turkish, everyone assumes that he is a good-for-nothing thug, and that his rebellious behaviour should be expected. The teachers at this school are constantly sending him to the principal's office without taking the slightest moment to consider the root of the problem.

Listen to me. I *know* the root of his problem. His father is the drug lord of Melbourne's prime criminal network. But he is gone now. He is out of Mick's life. For now. And there has got to be a way to inject some sense through Mick's thick emotionless skull. Should I stoop down to his level? Bully him? Use bad language? Would he respond to that? Obviously "power" doesn't faze him in the slightest. And who is to blame? Me? It is so easy for people to point the finger at the parents. But just look at Nash and Mia. Instead of getting worse after a family crisis, her attitude has gotten better, even if it *is* only on the surface. But that is one step in the right direction. There has got to be hope for Mick at some point.

"Mick," I half-whisper, adding a touch of grit from the rear of my throat, "what the *fuck* has gotten into you lately?" The taste of that rancid word contaminates my mouth like Mavala Stop—a polish to stop nail-biting, which my mother forced me to lick. I wasn't a nail-biter. But she wanted me to stop the biting, in general, so I'd make some Aussie friends.

For a very short instant, Mick looks taken aback, but then that devilish smirk of his melts into his cheeks like cream.

"Wow. That musta took some sorta effort." He sneers, puts his hands into his pockets, switches the weight from one foot to the other.

I, despite the intense uncertainty of using such language in the school corridor, am adamant not to be stepped all over. I grab him by the collar, push him to the wall, and attempt to lift him off the ground with one hand.

Not quite. Getting rusty?

I lower my voice to a guttural purr. "You disrespect anyone in my classroom again and I will show you what effort looks like, you hear?"

He laughs and nods repeatedly, feigning fright. I let go

of his collar and step back, keeping my posture upright, remaining impassive to his mockery.

"Just go home," I say, returning my voice back to normal. "There is food in the fridge." I straighten my shirtsleeve and avoid eye contact. "Drop by the nurse, tell her you are not feeling well."

Mick's bottom lip moves as if about to speak.

"Probably best you do not say anything else at this point," I say, crossing my arms in front of my chest. I point in the direction of the nurse's office, look at the floor, tap my foot, visualizing Ibrahim beating him to a pulp.

Darn it.

It all started when he saw the blood on the back porch. I am sure of it. Something changed in the way he'd look at me. As though he knew it wasn't an accident.

When I look up, he is gone.

I iron out the front of my skirt with my hands and step back into the classroom with a smile on my face. Two students are poking each other with the corners of their set squares. I groan under my breath.

It's the only downfall of being a mathematics teacher— my constant exposure to pointy objects.

chapter 7

mick

fuck her. fuck them all.

Forgot me fuckin' key. Again. Gotta go in through the back door. Again. Can't stand the back door. The first place me eyes go is the dark patch. It's not even that big. Me foot could probably cover it up. But it's there. And every time I see it, the memory zaps me between the fuckin' eyes, 'n' me head starts to pound with hate.

I don't even know who I hate.

I know it wasn't me mum's fault. She said she had to help clean it up. I remember it so fuckin' clearly. I didn't see nuthin' until it was just a stain. But I heard 'n' felt everythin'.

Me mum's squealin'.

Me dad's calm.

And then that fuckin' silence that lasted so long I swear to fuckin' God I thought they were both goners. I sat in the corner of me room. Tryin' not to cry. Because I knew that cryin' wasn't allowed.

I take a deep breath before I enter me house. 'Coz I know it looks like fuckin' shit bombed it, and it reeks like yobbo puke. Me mum keeps refusing to clean up until I start to "chip in."

I go inside and kick the bin outta me way. The kitchen looks like a fuckin' tornado hit it. If Mum comes home and it's still like this, she won't shut the fuck up about it.

I can hear her now, in that whiny fuckin' housewifey voice: *"If you enjoy living in a pigsty, then that's exactly what you'll get."*

But fuck her. Fuck everything.

All I want is Metallica. I turn it up. Earsplittin' loud.

And pray to Allah for everythin' to come good.

chapter 8

mia

can't i throw up in peace?

I spend recess in the toilets. I enter a cubicle, lift the plastic seat, and sit on the cold porcelain bowl. Just in case I crack the seat like last time. Not that I care about destroying school property. My pride? Maybe. After that shit with Mick I'm not sure I have much, but I'm sure as hell certain I'm gonna hold on to whatever I have left.

Yelling from the playground filters through the gap below the door—the gossip of girls whispering in front of the fractured mirror that's glued onto the beige brick like an afterthought; the yelling and screaming of wrestling boys, debating whose turn it is to fill the principal's fuel tank with water; basketballs bouncing against concrete walls, Anglo football jocks pretending they can dribble better than the black dudes who have already proved their status in the basketball tournament the previous week.

I spread my legs and lean forwards to open my schoolbag. My stomach pokes out from the bottom of my T-shirt and touches the cold toilet bowl. I know I shouldn't be doing this. But I can't help it. It's the only way I know how to self-medicate.

I pull out a Lamington. Shove the whole thing in my

mouth at once, squash it and swallow with barely a chew. I pull out another one. Shove that in too. I chew, mash, push the cake through my teeth with my eyes closed, making sure I can taste every single bit.

Because this is my last one.

Forever.

I promise.

When I swallow the last bit of Lamington stuck under my tongue, I feel a strange sense of relief.

I stand up and stare at the toilet bowl. I can do this.

I've seen how fast girls lose weight this way in those stupid '80s documentaries they play in Health class.

I zip up my bag, gulping pockets of air, deep and fast and heavy, to try to make myself feel sick. I feel a little dizzy and lean my shoulder against the right cubicle wall.

Let's do this.

I have to just do this. Not think about it. If I think about it, I'll back down. But I am thinking about it now, aren't I? Thinking about it by telling myself to not think about out.

Man . . .

I jam my fingers down my throat, convulse and heave as if I were vomiting the intestine of a cow. The whole thing has made me so ill that I keep dry-retching even when there is nothing left to spew. I close my eyes and my mouth, try to breathe through my nose to calm the hurricane in my stomach, to ease the throbbing in my temples.

Gross.

No way I'm doing this shit three times a day.

I knock the lid down, and it echoes like one of my mum's "motivational" cheek slaps.

I rip off some toilet paper to wipe my mouth, when someone knocks on my cubicle door.

The handle jiggles.

Silence.

Another knock.

"Leave me alone," I mumble. "I'm fine. It's just a stomach bug."

"No. It's not." The girl's voice is husky yet soft.

I straighten my back and look at the gap at the bottom of the door. The girl's presence hovers in a shadow.

Is she serious? "And how the fuck would you know that?"

The girl shifts her feet. The tip of her sneaker peeks through the bottom of the door.

"I can help you lose weight."

What the hell? "Huh?"

"Just open the door. It's Kimiko. I'm alone."

chapter 9

nash
it's all celeste's fault

During recess, I sit at my desk to play FIFA 13, sweaty and hot after joining the boys in a rough game of basketball. The girls were whiny today, so I just let them sit on the sidelines to file each other's nails. Except one girl who insisted she "get down and dirty." The honorary boy of the class, who I want to help apply for an AIS scholarship. For a moment I wish I had a daughter like her, then withdraw the thought, queasy with guilt.

Teachers' footsteps fill the staff room with the mental weight of dealing with classroom misbehaviour, their noses in manila folders, fingers hooked around cups of coffee, as they walk by my desk. Thank crikey for the cubicles. If it wasn't for this antisocial static mass of plywood everybody complains about, it would be damn impossible to chill out here. At all. "Sometimes goodness comes in mysterious ways." Yeah, Celeste was right about that. She was often right about a lot of things.

She was right about Mia too.

I glance at the time in the bottom-right-hand corner of my screen. Sonia should be back any minute. I open my drawer and pull out a pear. As I bite into it, I catch sight of my Drum. And groan.

I should quit. Mia and I should quit our addictions together. It would give her something to nag me about at the same time. Maybe it would help her. I did force a lot of fruit onto her this morning, but for all I know, she's chucked it in the bin and bought junk with the cash Celeste keeps putting into her bank account. Guilt money.

How the hell am I supposed to help Mia like this?

Sure, Celeste's heart might be in the right place. But she doesn't know about Mia's gaining weight. It's been over a year since she's seen her.

Gotta tell her.

Mia will kill me.

It's for her own good.

"You are kidding me. FIFA?" Sonia knocks me over my head with a stack of papers.

"Ow! The principal should file those papers as a prohibited weapon," I say.

Sonia snorts and rolls a chair over from another cubicle. She rests her papers in her lap and folds her hands on top of them with a tight-lipped smile.

"We must talk."

I smirk and wobble my head as I pause the game before facing her.

"Sounds serious."

"Cut it out." Sonia squints.

"Ah." I nod and scratch my beard. "You mean *serious* serious."

Sonia looks into her lap and licks her lips. My left foot starts to twitch.

"Okay, out with it. What she do now?"

Sonia shakes her head. "It is not what she has done. It is what she is not doing. She has stopped sticking up for herself, Nash. She used to be so confident and outspoken, rude sometimes, but rude was better than *this*—"

"I'll speak to her," I say, and face my computer again.

"Nash. Look at me." Sonia emphasizes her words with a couple of knuckle-knocks on my desk.

"Sonia. Look—" I clench my teeth, take a deep breath, hold it for a second, and let it out with my next words. "I can't get through to her. I've tried and tried and tried to get her to stick to a diet. I even suggested forking out some cash to get her stomach stapled, but she—"

"Her stomach stapled? Oh, I—" Sonia hangs her head in her hands.

"What?"

"You suggested *what*?"

"I—"

"No, no, no!"

I crane my neck a little and pucker my brow.

"You might as well have told her she was not good enough."

I *tsk*. "Nah."

Sonia sighs. "Someone spat at her in class this morning, and she hardly even flinched. She wiped it off her face with her sleeve and just got back to work. It was as if she thought she deserved it."

I roll my seat back a few inches and rub my hands over my face. "Which little shithead was it?"

"It does not matter. I have dealt with the kid. Now you need to deal with Mia."

I nod and sniff.

Sonia pokes me in my chest with her index finger. "Tonight."

"I will."

"I mean it."

"I know, mate. I said I will, alright?"

Sonia looks at her feet. "What are you going to say?"

"Don't know. I'll think of something."

Sonia squeezes my knee and stands up. "Just going to fetch a coffee, and I will be right back."

I nod, watch Sonia walk out, stare in the direction she left, in some sort of trance. I *will* say something to Mia tonight.

Right after I've spoken to Celeste.

chapter 10

mia

to take or not to take

I've never spoken to Kimiko before. You know, I can't even remember seeing *her* speak to anyone since year seven. And the only time I've ever heard her name was from the roll call in last year's Social Studies class.

Once.

But I remember her nevertheless. Because every time I pass her in the schoolyard she looks like she's in some sort of Japanese punk music clip, looking thoughtfully towards nothingness, ciggie lodged in the corner of her mouth that never seems to go out, dressed in something like black faded skinny jeans, a purple Sonic Youth T-shirt, and dark-grey Converses. Kimiko should be in the collage on my bedroom door, not smoking ciggies in this shithole high school pretending not to exist.

The shadow of Kimiko's foot lingers a little longer by my cubicle door before I open it. I open the door, and she's staring right at me. Her black eyes stand out against her pale skin and dark silky hair like black diamonds in white sand. Envy darts through my chest. God, I wish I looked like her. That exotic beauty is rare. Especially in this school rampant with the offspring of white trailer trash.

Why didn't I ever notice how pretty she was?

Because you were a slut-face bitch, remember?

In silence, Kimiko swivels round to reach into her back pocket, and her T-shirt shifts slightly upwards and reveals a scar along her hip bone, jagged, bumpy, not at all a clean cut.

I want to touch it.

Kimiko holds out a small Ziploc bag of pills. "Here."

I stare at them, eyes locked on to the bag like a magnet. My top lip twitches. Kimiko laughs and scratches the corner of her mouth with her ring finger, her bitten nails painted a deep matte maroon.

"No biggie, hun. Just caffeine." Kimiko smirks and tilts her head to the side. Her Cleopatra fringe sits firmly in place.

Sure, I used to be the school slut, but I have never touched drugs before. Maybe they're only caffeine, but to take them on purpose freaks me out a little. But I shouldn't turn them down. It would be rude. Right?

Yeah, man, keep telling yourself that.

I snatch the bag off Kimiko and push the small white pills around the plastic with my thumb. The bag is new. As if she had packaged them especially. Maybe she's a dealer. Wouldn't surprise me.

"And these are gonna help me lose weight?" I say, my tone rising a little too high at the end of the question. I must sound like such a dork.

"Yeah. Just make sure you drink lots of water." Kimiko

squeezes her petite fingers into her tight pockets so her knuckles are still showing. Her elbows stick out like flamingo knees. She flicks her head, as if trying to remove hair from her face, and raises her brow. A cue for me to respond, I guess, but I'm tongue-tied. I don't want the drugs, but I don't want to lose the opportunity to form a new friendship either. She might be my last chance at having a decent go of my final year in high school.

The end of recess bell rings. Some kid outdoors curses and bounces a ball; it echoes through the entrance of the toilet block.

Kimiko winks and flicks her head in the direction of the exit as if to say *let's go*. My mouth is half open, ready to speak, unable to voice my thoughts. "Thank you" somehow doesn't seem right—neither does silence.

Kimiko shrugs with a tight-lipped smile and turns to leave.

"Um—" I sniff.

She pauses and spins round, lifting one foot off the ground and balancing it on the tip of her shoe. She stares. Her nostrils flare.

Say something.

"Don't worry." Kimiko smiles, twisting her hair into a bun and immediately letting it drop loose. It falls in front of her shoulder like liquid. "Start with one. See how you feel."

See how I feel?

"How . . . will I feel?"

"Not much." Kimiko laughs.

I look at the pills cradled in my palm. The bag is getting clammy. Sweat pools below the plastic.

"You'll probably feel normal."

"Normal," I repeat, trying to make sense of what that actually means.

"Yeah. Normal." Kimiko shrugs.

I drop the pills into the side pocket of my bag and zip it shut, the *zzz* sound becoming one with the voices outside.

"We'd better get to class," Kimiko says.

"Wait! Do you wanna, um—" I look at my feet.

Should I?

Kimiko frowns and crosses her arms with friendly impatience.

"Wanna do something later?" I blurt out, feeling my face flush.

Kimiko pouts and says with a curt nod, "Meet you here at lunch."

I smile. Thank, God. First non-rejection in months.

Together we walk out of the toilet block, separated by a metre of space, teeming with untapped energy.

By the afternoon it becomes an inch, and she lets me call her Kimi.

chapter 11

sonia

is this how you be a mother?

I stand on my doorstep, briefcase in hand, staring at our brass knocker, its lion head roaring at me to smarten up. The wind blows my blouse flat against my back as I look at the round overgrown patch of grass where I attempted to landscape a mini rock garden last year. The pile of decorative pebbles are now lost in weeds, and the tiny apricot tree struggles to survive on its own, producing one apricot a year, as if too stubborn to be conquered by human neglect. Every time I return home, I am sure I can hear the tree spitting at me: *"You never learn, do you, woman?"*

I do not want to go inside. I never want to go inside. He is waiting for me. Ready to pounce, either with degrading comments or silence; I do not know which is worse. But I have got to stop doing this. Working late every night is not going to fix the relationship between us. It is not going to fix *me*.

As I insert my key, the sound of a car screeching and crashing leaps from the open living room window. He has left the fly-wire off. Again.

"Fuck you, you motherfuckin' wanker-fuck!" he screams. "Cunt!"

Something falls to the floor and thick thuds follow, a bit of bookcase abuse, perhaps. The roar of the digital explosion stops abruptly. He must have turned off the TV.

I open the door slowly enough for the hinges not to squeak. I step inside and place my briefcase delicately by the door as I do every night—easy access for the next morning. No. The real reason is I hope Mick will open it and find the journal I leave in there. Read all about my struggles. Maybe he will feel sorry for me and realize how hard life has been with his father. Maybe he will realize he's had me wrapped around his little finger, and I had no choice.

Maybe the journal is a complete and utter lie I am trying to make myself believe I am not responsible for my actions.

I can still . . . taste the pleasure. That thrill when the knife slips in and the blood oozes like liquid velvet.

I envision the look of calm on a dead face, relax my jaw, and take a deep breath. I adjust the cuffs and collar of my blouse and push my hair behind my ears. Keeping up appearances, even at home, is important for my rehabilitation.

I stride down the hallway, head high, towards the kitchen. My son's shadow ripples over the tiled floor as I approach the arched entranceway. The fridge door opens and closes. Its contents rattle like the music of water-filled crystal glasses. Along with a running bath, it is perhaps the only other relaxing sound I ever hear in this household.

"Fuckin' bitch fuckin' ate it." Mick scoffs, snorts, coughs, spits into the sink. It splatters like fresh fish gut.

I lean against the archway, fold my arms under my breasts, and try to drill a hole through Mick's head with a glare. I am going to have to tackle this with a little less "nice." I have been trying so hard. To be a good mum. To get this family back on track. But maybe I've got the balance wrong.

So I just say it.

"What did the fucking bitch fucking eat, Mick?" I raise my eyebrows, trying to maintain my assertiveness from the morning.

He looks up and smirks, shoves a hand down the front of his jeans, and rearranges his package. I look him up and down. Mick winks, spits into the sink again, and walks out without uttering another word.

"You did not just walk away from me," I call towards the ceiling, trying to disguise my tears with volume. "You come back and apologize. And apologize for this morning in class."

Mick's bedroom door slams, and the boom of heavy metal sucks the oxygen out of the house. This is a prison. And I built it myself. But how could I have possibly done any better? I have been the perfect textbook mother since Ibrahim left. Is it the lack of a sane father that has done this? If only I could get him to see someone, to *talk* to someone, then maybe we'd have a chance.

I pull out a chair and sit down. The kitchen bench and sink is overflowing with dirty dishes. There's something pink and sticky that smells like cough syrup all over the floor by the dishwasher and broken brown glass sitting mercilessly at the base of the garbage bin.

I cry. My shoulders shake, and my throat constricts from the effort of keeping quiet. I am *sick*, I think. The chaos that was this household before my husband left was the only thing that kept me sane when my parents died. Especially when Mick said he couldn't wait until I followed suit.

I wipe my eyes with the heels of my hands, prop a shiny carving knife on the windowsill above the sink, and glance at it now and again, while I clear away the mess.

chapter 12

nash

she would, wouldn't she?

As the chicken breasts grill, I prepare a salad, wondering where Mia is. It's been months since she's been late home from school. I was all hyped to have that talk. But now my confidence has waned.

I couldn't bring myself to call Celeste either. What's got into me? Crikey. Have I become that much of a wuss? I'm a father to a beautiful young woman, and I can't even bring myself to talk to her about something that surely worries her as much as it does me. She's quite mature for her age sometimes, and she can probably handle it, but I feel like all I'm good for nowadays is putting my nose in where it's not wanted.

I think seriously about what Sonia said in the staff room as I chop lettuce into paper-thin strips. In the back of my mind, Celeste nags that I'm going to cause the leaves to oxidize. *Who gives a . . . ?* Would Mia really think I'm trying to help her lose weight because I'm ashamed of the way she looks? I reckon she'd understand I just want what's best for her. Sonia has to be overreacting, speaking from her own insecurities. Why do the skinny ones lack more self-confidence than the overweight ones?

Mia hasn't shown any signs of resentment towards me. Has she? She always seems so much angrier at herself than she does at me. Which is a good thing. Wait. No. That can't be a good thing at all—

Mia flings the front door open. It ricochets off the arm of the couch and slams shut. She throws her schoolbag at the foot of the coffee table and runs to her room without a glance in my direction. Her footsteps rumble in my stomach like a bad meal.

"Dinner. Ten minutes," I call out, groaning at her inability to be human and at my inability to act natural around her. I always feel like I'm putting on an act, being the boring, responsible parent, trying to "do the right thing," when all I really want to do is be her best mate, take her to the footy, order ham and pineapple pizza, pig out on burgers. Shit like that.

This is fucked. I can't even offer her a big juicy steak!

Silence.

Footsteps on floorboards in the hallway.

Door handle squeak.

Slam.

Something hits the floor.

Stereo full blast. Magic Dirt: "I Was Cruel." It's the only song I ever hear anymore.

I smile sadly as nostalgia pulses in my temples. I dice the last cucumber, chuck it into the salad bowl.

I squat to take a gander at the chicken under the grill. The intense dry heat radiates across my forehead and stings my eyes.

I'll give it a couple.

I stand, wash my hands, and lean my back against the counter, wiping my hands dry on my T-shirt. I look out the kitchen window and say to myself, "We're doing alright. I'm doing the best I can."

I am, aren't I? I can't tell anymore. But the more I let myself feel guilty for wondering if I'm doing a good job or not, the more I feel like I'm not doing a good job. I reckon I have to count myself lucky that she's a decent human being with a kind heart. Even if she often tries to hide it.

Mia surfaces from the hermit's cave she likes to call her bedroom when I pull the chicken out of the grill and leave the tray on the stove.

Is the universe being friendly to me tonight, or is it some sort of test? Usually I would have to knock on Mia's door over and over before she showed her face. By then, her food would be cold, and I would be accused of being an incompetent father. I would defend myself, make sure Mia knew it was her own fault the food was cold. And then she'd retaliate with, "You know I take ages. You should start calling me twenty minutes before you actually wanna serve."

You can't beat that logic, I reckon.

Mia approaches the kitchen counter with a grin.

"You okay?" I say.

Mia *tsks*.

"Okay, stupid question." I'm about to ask why she's so cheery, but then realize I might be pushing it. Maybe I should save the interrogation for later. Or maybe I won't even need to talk to her after all. She seems so much better than she was in the morning.

"Nice to see your teeth for a change." I wince at my unintentional sarcasm, bracing myself for back talk. I put away a few dry dishes to avoid eye contact. There I go again. I should be awarded wuss of the year.

"Lucky I've been using your whitening stuff, then," Mia says.

I laugh and scratch my beard, half on the verge of getting shitty about her using my toothpaste, and half pleasantly surprised that she thought to look after her appearance. That's got to be a good sign.

I slide the bowl of salad towards Mia and point to the chicken breasts resting on the stove. "You can serve yourself today."

Mia grabs a plate, fills it to the brim with salad, and puts half a chicken breast on the side. I watch in silent satisfaction, grab myself a plate of food, switch on the TV, and slump into the couch.

"Weather's nice. Gonna eat in the backyard," Mia says.

I stand. "Good idea."

"Um. Alone."

"Oh." I sit again and nod. "Go for it."

"Sorry." Mia screws up her nose as if she might be feeling guilty. "I just want to . . . you know . . . think."

"Yep." I salute. "Understood." I do understand. But I can't deny I feel a twinge of rejection. I reckon I just have to accept that I'm never going to be her mate. A father is a father, and always a father.

Mia shakes her head. "You're such a dick."

"Thanks. Your compliments always bring a tear to my eye."

"Anytime." Mia stands there, plate in one hand, a glass of water in the other. She stares at me with a strange smirk on her face. I'm happy she seems happier today, but was it brought on by something? And how has the incident in class not gotten her down?

"Mia. Go. I'm fine. Wanna watch *7:30 Report* anyway," I say. It's true.

Mia blinks, as if she's just snapped out of a trance. "Yep," she says, and walks out dragging her tattered and grimy tracksuit cuffs along the carpet.

I flick to the ABC and pull the coffee table between my knees. Footage of a school trip gone troppo in Echuca with kids smoking and shooting up, drinking copious amounts of booze, and getting arrested flashes over the TV screen. I cut off a piece of chicken and put it in my mouth; chewing and chuckling at the memory of being a bit of a teen rebel myself, at Celeste and me smoking pot, getting drunk, having sex in the back of my father's E-Type Jag while it was parked in the garage right next to my parents' bedroom.

God, it was fun trying to be so quiet.

Crikey, C. We really pulled the wool over their eyes, you and me.

I laugh out loud and chew with my mouth open.

Then my chewing slows. I rest my knife and fork on the edge of my plate.

Swallow.
Rub my hands over my face.
Squint at the TV, elbows resting on my knees.
I sway side to side a little. Then hang my head.
Oh, Mia.
Suddenly, I feel sick.
She wouldn't be doing anything stupid, would she?

chapter 13

sonia

it is simply a safety net

The phone rings. A welcome distraction. But how can I hear anything with Mick's metal blaring like it is the end of the world? I lift the receiver off the wall and hold it to my right ear. I stick a finger in my left to block out the music.

"Hello?" I say, trying not to shout.

"Sonia, it's Nash."

"Oh hi. Sorry about the racket, but I cannot do much about it at this point. Do you want to call back later?"

"No worries, I'll be quick."

I nod and pinch the skin between my eyes. "Is everything okay?"

"Mia's behaviour is—uh, I want to get your opinion about something. Can we meet?"

I sigh with relief. Any excuse to get out. Any excuse that isn't my own flight-before-fight syndrome.

"Sure. Dexter's in Northcote?"

"Half an hour?"

"See you soon."

I hang up, load the dishwasher, put the knife I was ogling back in the drawer, and slip on a pair of blue jeans that are hanging on the clotheshorse. On my way out I apply a bit of red lipstick in the hallway mirror, take a handful of cash from my briefcase and put it in my back pocket.

As I step outside, I decide once and for all that the next time Ibrahim turns up on my doorstep, my pistol will be within reach.

chapter 19

mia

can i just squeeze my eyes shut and pretend i'm being responsible?

I sit on the wooden bench in the backyard. The one my mother insisted go under the fig tree so she could read her fitness magazines in the afternoon shade. Pain in the arse, this bench. Rotten gunk that looks like decaying organs sticks to it twice a year. And I'm always left to clean it up. The spatula used to scrape the rotting flesh off the not-so-varnished-anymore bench is jammed in the dirt at the base of the tree's trunk—its dark-green-tinted handle faded at the tip, where the sun hits it every morning. I can't help but think it looks like a moldy penis-zombie escaping from its grave.

Doesn't help that Dad doesn't give a toss about collecting the figs to eat, either. Or the garden. The only time he ever sat out here to "read," was the day Mum left. His reading material? His own desperate text messages that he never got replies for.

I rest my plate of food and water by my right thigh and try to cross my legs, but it hurts my knees, pulls the skin so tight that it stings. So I sit like a bloke with a stubby of beer hanging between his legs. It's a position I'd like to stop sitting in, but it's the most comfortable.

When I was skinny, this position looked sexy. I had attitude; the boys drooled. Well . . . I like to think they drooled, especially when I licked ciggie papers, pinched my tobacco, and lit them, tautly rolled, with one eye half-squinted. But now I just look like a desperate, attention-seeking fat girl.

How did I let myself get like this? What was I trying to prove?

A tear escapes the corner of my eye. It tickles my cheek. I wipe it away, checking that Dad isn't spying on me through the back window.

I slip the Ziploc bag of caffeine pills out of my back pocket and fiddle with them like beads in plastic. If I take one now, will I stay up all night and burn some hard-core calories? You know, just to give the whole process a decent kick start, then I'll be good. If I can stay awake as much as possible, it's only logical that the weight should start dropping off. Right?

I don't know, man. Honestly? What if I'm allergic?

I put the pills back in my pocket and stare at my plate, at the chicken fillet balancing on the edge. I pick it up, sniff it. Its salty fragrance makes my mouth water. But I shouldn't. So I squeeze my eyes shut and fling it behind my shoulders and over the fig tree. A flock of birds fly away as it hits the back fence.

I shove in a few mouthfuls of salad and chew quickly. One of the lettuce stalks tickles the back of my throat and makes my gag.

Should I see what Kimi is doing tonight? I don't wanna

come off clingy. Maybe it would be better to wait till tomorrow. Now that I've lost my popularity, I don't have my posse. I know they weren't real friends, but at least it looked like I had some. I feel like Kimi is the only chance I have left at finding out what a real friend is.

I close my eyes. The rustle of leaves and the light breeze brushes over my skin.

I can do this. I have the willpower.

I stand, walk over to the compost heap near back fence, and dump the rest of my salad into it.

No food.

I know. It's a stupid idea. But just one night. I need a decent head start to boost my confidence.

I pull the bag of pills out of my pocket again, sit down, and pop one into my mouth.

Just a kick start. A few days.

I promise not to become a statistic.

chapter 15

nash

if only parents had a bedroom

I sit outside at Dexter's despite the wind picking up speed. I light a pre-rolled cigarette, take a long drag, and nod a thank-you as the waiter brings me my double Maker's Mark. Neat.

I reckon the café bar is pretty quiet for a Thursday night. The weather is off-kilter, but what's new for Melbourne?

On the opposite side of the street, I spot a young dude drinking from a VB stubby, and smoking. It looks too thick for a cigarette. Probably a joint. His dirty fluoro-green baseball cap hides his eyes. On the corner of the block is a cop car. Waiting. Eyeing the dude. The fluoro-dude spits, drags, breathes, swigs, paces. Spits, drags, breathes, swigs, pulls a knife out of his pocket, inspects it, smiles, puts it back in his pocket. Paces. The cops don't seem to notice as he pisses off around the corner.

His gait and build remind me of Ibrahim at that age. My stomach tenses up. To think he almost convinced me to be a partner in his new "business" venture. Crikey. I can only imagine what would have become of me. If I'd've become anything at all. I reckon I'd be dead in a ditch. Or someone's back yard. Or maybe I'd have been done on Sonia's back porch.

"Did you talk to her?"

Sonia's voice snaps me out of my trance. She steps onto the curb and pulls out her seat. It scrapes on the concrete. She winces, shivers, then rubs her bare goose-bumpy arms. As she sits down, she squashes her hands between her knees, eyes the waiter to come and take her order. I flare my nostrils, take a sip of my drink and swish it around my mouth. The waiter swaggers out with an unhealthily large grin on his pink freckled face. Sonia mimics his expression in jest and orders what I have.

It's our usual.

If it wasn't for Sonia's red lips and the deep smile lines around her big black eyes, she'd look like a schoolgirl right now. I don't know what I'd do without Sonia in my life. She always makes me feel so much lighter. Which is weird, considering.

I wonder what life would have been like if I'd married her instead of Celeste? Sonia pretty much kept to herself in high school. At least until she hooked up with Ibrahim. But now that I look back, even though I never said anything to him, I'm sure the fucker only hit on her because he knew I'd set my eyes on her first. I s'pose at the time it just made sense. Because of their nationality and all. So I never challenged it. I moved on to the next-best-looking chick and that was it.

Our futures marked in stone.

Sonia shakes her head and blinks numerous times. "What happened to the weather? This stinks."

"I reckon that was summer," I say. I lean back in my seat and spread my legs.

"Half of it was overcast. We should move to the Gold Coast. You and me. And leave the kids to fend for themselves?"

I'm not sure how to react to that. So I take another sip of my bourbon in silence. Sonia laughs and flicks her hand in the air. For a moment there I thought she was serious.

"Well?" Sonia asks, craning her neck.

"What?"

"The talk?"

"Nope," I say, and take a long drag on my cigarette.

"Nash!"

"That's what I wanted to talk about."

"I am not doing it for you."

"Not gonna ask you that."

Sonia squints at me. The corner of her mouth twists upwards.

"Mia is—" I sip my bourbon as if I'm trying to eat the glass. "Really *happy* today."

"And?"

"You know, smiling, being nice, no back talk. She sat in the backyard to 'think.'" I pause for a moment and let smoke ooze from my nose. "And ate *salad*. On her own." I shift in my seat and glance at Sonia's feet. She's wearing thongs; her toenails are painted bright pink. I realize I've never noticed her crooked toes before. A couple even look like Twisties.

"Teenagers tend to want to be on their own," Sonia says, as if reading it out of a manual.

My mouth goes dry. I soothe it with another swig of bourbon. "Do you think she's hiding stuff?" I say *stuff* in such a way that means it mightn't be harmless. One thing is for sure—Mia's behaviour is out of character. And sudden. I reckon I'd be fooling myself to think otherwise.

"Teenagers always hide stuff from their parents." Again she speaks in that monotone teacher's voice.

The waiter brings out Sonia's drink. She winks a thank-you. Another sudden shift in attitude. It's like her real self is finding little opportunities to show its face. Maybe she needs this drink as much as I do. The waiter blushes and walks backwards into the empty table next to us. Sonia and I smile at each other and pretend not to notice.

"Look." Sonia cups her bourbon like a mug of coffee and closes her eyes with a deep breath. She holds it in. As she slowly exhales, it blends with the whoosh of cars—they sound different in the dark, like they're passing through thick air, unfriendly and sad.

"If you ignore your gut," Sonia says, with her eyes still shut, "you are neglecting them. If you ask too many questions, you are being overprotective. If you try to be friends with them, you are an embarrassment. If you are strict, they rebel. If you are lenient, they take advantage. If—"

"Sonia." I scoff. I get it. We can't win. But she's supposed to be the one that *knows*.

She opens her eyes and forces a crooked smile.

"Just tell me what *you* would do." I lean forwards and rest my arms on the table. "Be honest with me."

She shifts her gaze across the street. Her smile fades and her eyes glaze over. The fluoro-dude is back, pacing up and down the street again, with a new bottle of booze in one hand and the knife in the other. Sonia squints at him, glances over at the oblivious cops. Pity plays with her gentle face. I'm pretty sure I know what she's thinking about.

"I'd . . . ," Sonia whispers, still staring at the guy across the road. "I wouldn't second-guess myself. Regardless of the consequences. Even if I would end up with blood on my hands."

chapter 16

celeste
from fit to fake to freak

Karter's taking on a pro bono surgery. I cackle within. Oh my God, what a joke. Okay, okay, I was the one who convinced him to do it by reminding him of the positive publicity and reputation boost. Can you blame me? The money is fab. And so is the spotlight. But I never knew he would do this to me. Force me under the knife. My passion is *getting* into shape, not cutting into shape. But what could I do? It was either suffer through the drop and fluff, or be ditched for a younger, thinner, more beautiful me.

"Karter, honey?" I bare my teeth—a smile in his eyes—and quickly pin up my hair before holding a pair of earrings to my ears. "What do you think of these with my new tan?" I spin around on my five-inch heels, flicking my hip to the side, jutting out my newly-healed boob job. I feel sexy in this black Prada gown, all set for tonight's gala, but what's the point in wearing $20,000 if he doesn't even notice it? His eyes go straight to my tits. Of course. He's admiring his handiwork.

Karter peers above a pair of invisible spectacles and offers a gentle grin—the one that frequently contradicts his true colours when manipulating a patient into having an unnecessary procedure. I see it all the time. Does he really think I don't notice when he tries it on me?

"They look divine." Karter nods and pinches something off the tip of his tongue. He frowns at a selection of X-rays spread across our bed, shifts a few around. "But if you'd gotten that Botox to accentuate your cheekbones, they'd probably look even better." He taps his nose.

"Oh." I nod and swallow. My smile deflates. Sure, it was fake. But sometimes pretending makes it seem real. I guess there's no need to cover my emotional wounds anymore. Karter wouldn't know the difference between genuine hurt and a playful Botox pout.

"Well, I'll leave my hair down for tonight, then?"

Karter's top lip twitches with his brief nod of acceptance, and he steps inside his five-metre-long closet.

"Wouldn't want to draw too much attention to my shapeless face," I whisper in the mirror, squinting at Karter behind my own reflection. He is sorting through his row of dark-grey tuxedos. He insists they each have their own unique style to suit his mood. I can hardly tell the difference between the grey, the black, and the "Prussian" blue, let alone those of identical colour.

I unclip my hair. It unravels over my right breast, hangs, motionless—a taunting silky tragedy. I brush it one last time before putting on my powder-pink lippy. Estée Lauder. Honestly? I miss the good old Body Shop on Bourke Street.

I open my panty drawer and rummage for my stash of Xanax, despite promising myself that I'd no longer self-medicate. I haven't taken one in three months. I've been a really good girl. At Karter's beck and call. Making sure the housemaids' work hours are in order so we don't end up paying for the two of them at once. Really? Who cares! Karter has enough money to pay the wages of every housemaid in America and still retire a billionaire.

Maybe if I set things straight with Nash once and for all I'll feel better about myself. I would get some closure. And I could also convince Mia to come and live with me here. But how could I possibly tell Nash I've been lying to him all these years without some chemical courage? Especially since the lie is going to be a lie.

I'm so lonely! What choice do I have? I made such a huge mistake marrying Karter. But there's no chance of going back to my old life by asking politely. They hate my guts. It's lie to Nash, or die alone and plastic.

I twist the cap off the bottle of Xanax and shake a couple of pills into my palm.

I imagine they are little people eating out of my hand. So cute!

"It's time," I whisper to the pills. "It's time to tell him it was Ibrahim."

chapter 17

mia
whoa

I lie flat on my back. On my bedroom floor. Eyelashes pinned to my eyebrows. The rough red rug Sonia brought for me from Turkey prickles my upper thighs. It's a perfect reminder that the mass of skin on my body is growing, and that I'm doing the right thing by taking these pills.

Despite its periodic nature, the traffic is loud. Too loud. Too present. The whoosh of wheels along the wet road wavers; white noise hangs around my body like tangible clouds. The rhythm of my breath encompasses the room, the midnight air now sticky from the unexpected storm, the temperature change a sign of something . . .

. . . not right.

I turn to my side, grab the edge of my bed, and pull myself off the floor. I push my tongue into my front teeth as though it might help me keep balanced. My knees crack and my heart pounds, rises, thumps in my throat. My head feels so light it's as if it's not even there, the air soft on my skin. I grab my phone off my desk and text Kimi: *Don't feel good.*

I pace the room.

The floorboards creak, and I wonder if I'm gonna need

Dad, I don't wanna need Dad, it would be embarrassing, he'd stop trusting me, I'd have to lose weight the normal way, and not at all quickly enough to be skinny for when Mum comes home, she could visit at any time, she could be here tomorrow, she said she was coming at the end of summer, it's past the end of summer, she must be coming soon, fuck, she can't see me like this, shit, imagine if she saw me like this? Dad pushed her away by just being the man he is . . . what's Mum gonna think now that I'm a big fat fucking cow?

My phone buzzes.

"Hey!" I say so loud my voice vibrates through my head.

"You're not freaking out on me, are you?" Kimi's voice is slow, calm, soothing. I stop dead in the middle of my room, close my eyes, and take a long deep breath through my nose. All I want to do is talk. But I would sound ridiculous. And what if Dad came home? He'd hear me babbling and wonder what was going on. I don't need that right now.

Don't.

Need it.

"I took two," I say, and sit on the edge of my bed. A spring snaps and throbs through the mattress.

"You what? Jesus."

"You said they were just caffeine!"

Silence. Fuck fuck fuck fuck . . .

"Kimi, please—"

"If I'd told you they were uppers, you probably wouldn't have taken them."

"Uppers? I'm on— What the fuck is an upper?"

"Speed, Mia. You're on speed."

Oh my God. I look out my window, as if the cops are gonna come charging in to arrest me at any second.

Kimi laughs—deep, velvety. Suddenly I forget about the cops and think about kissing her.

I blink. Hard. Whoa.

Now I feel calm. But it only lasts a short moment. "Why did you want me to take speed?"

"Was a test."

"Why?" I squeal, then slam my hand over my mouth. Why am I speaking so loudly?

"Hey, Mia?"

"What?"

"You're gonna be fine."

"Um . . . can you please just tell me what's going on?"

Kimi sighs; something muffles the receiver. I can hear tapping, and saliva swishing around Kimi's mouth as if she's sucking on a lollypop. My crotch tingles.

Holy fuck, why am I so turned on and so freaked out at the same time?

"Um. I needed to test you."

"Needed?"

"Yep."

"Did I pass?" What am I talking about?

"A-ha."

It starts to rain again. It patters on the windowpane like a sweet lullaby. I stare at my reflection in the glass and tip my head to the side. My mascara has smudged.

Pretty.

"Mia?" Kimi asks, her voice rising in tone a little. "I need your help with something. I need to you to help me fuck someone up. Can I trust you?"

chapter 18

sonia

did i really say "lemme?"

I have had three double bourbons on a school night. Nash has had five, and has almost finished his packet of Drum. He is rolling his last slither of tobacco now, grinning like an idiot. A handsome one, though. And an awkwardly charming one.

I am a lucky woman.

The street spins around me like a Google map virtual view, in a slow and beautiful cinematographic glide. No nausea, just a sluggish yet embraced lull in my tired and abused brain. It has been a long time since I felt the effects of alcohol, and it is absolutely splendid. I can still hold it down pretty well. Remarkable really. Even more remarkable that I think it is something to be proud of. But I am. Especially in front of Nash, who is still grinning like an idiot, lighting his cigarette, staring into the sky, exhaling his smoke as if a sacrifice to the moon. The man on the moon. I like to think of him as God—an optical illusion, something we *wish* to perceive.

"What do you think of God?" I say with a few too many pauses between words. I mark the end of the question with a mouthful of bourbon. Or perhaps it is to prevent myself from vomiting more nonsense.

"Not a bad guy." Nash takes another drag. "Met him at the pub last weekend." He exhales with a smirk. A short gust of wind shifts his cap, but he pulls it back down before it comes off.

"Since when do you go and see live music?" I say.

"I don't."

I frown and draw my chin into my neck. A bubble of vomit rises up my throat, but I catch it just in time and swallow it back down with a wince.

I squint at Nash, with my head tilted to the side. I feel sixteen again. The day I tried to act cool in front of him in Chemistry. I recited the periodic table from top to bottom, after looking at it for only two minutes. I saw Nash smile at me. I thought he was going to say something, but Ibrahim slapped him on the back and started whispering about getting high behind the shelter shed at lunch. I will never forget how much I wanted to be invited. I will also never forget how much I regret being invited the next day.

My face is hot, the tips of my fingers cold, my palms and feet sweaty. I fling my head back and look into the sky—the stars are hidden behind a thick mass of grey cloud illuminated by the city's glow.

"I said *God*. Do you believe in him?" I look back down and clear my throat.

Nash squashes his top lip to his nose in thought, takes another sip of his drink using the hand that is holding the cigarette.

"Actually, do not answer that. Lemme ask you another question." Wow. Was that a slur? Did I really just say *lemme*?

Nash taps his cigarette on the edge of the ashtray. It's the first time the wind hasn't blown the ash away.

Nash looks into my eyes; the streetlights reflect off them like travelling souls. I count the seconds of silence in my head and divide it by pi—just for fun.

"What would you say if I said I was serious about the Gold Coast?" I soften and lower my voice, trying not to sound drunk. "It is their last year of school; they can look after themselves."

Nash smiles and gets the waiter's attention. He asks for the bill.

"What are you doing?" I say. Why does he keep ignoring me? Are we leaving? I was just beginning to relax. I need this. I have needed it for a long, long time. I am not done. Need another drink, but I do not have the energy to protest. I look at my hands, all four of them, blurring into each other.

Nash smirks at me, lifts his pelvis, pulls his wallet out of his back pocket, slams it on the table like a deck of cards.

I laugh and down the remainder of my drink. I close my eyes and sigh.

School. Right. Forgot for a moment. That was nice.

The waiter arrives with the bill. Nash pays, shoves my hand away when I try to pay my share. Nash stands, holds out his hand to help me out of my seat. I put my hand in his. He pulls lightly, and I float to my feet. I fall into him, the top of my head on his chest, supporting the weight of my body. Both arms hang limp by my side. Nash kisses the top of my head and breathes into my hair like it's a secret.

We stand, joined brain to heart. In silence.

"Can I please stay with you tonight?" I whisper.

Nash flicks his cigarette onto the road, levers me into a standing position, and takes my hand. He leads me towards his car.

For a very brief moment, I wonder what it would feel like to stab him.

chapter 19

nash
she's her mother's daughter

The bourbon just hit me. Great example I am. For my daughter. Drunk driver. Smoker. Pizza-eater. All hidden behind the mask of a Physical Education teacher. Crikey. I got a lot going for me, don't I? I promise myself I won't do it again. But I reckon I will. It's just the nature of being human, I s'pose. The single-dad status could also be my downfall. But the calming effect of the alcohol makes me feel like my life is great. In this moment. Nothing to worry about. At least not until the morning.

By the time I roll into my driveway, Sonia is fast asleep, clutching a bottle of water to her chest. Her face is squashed against the passenger window, mouth open wide, a cone-shaped mist painting the glass like the voice of a ghost. I turn off the ignition. The car rumbles to a halt.

I admire Sonia's beauty in the after-hush of the engine growl. Her eyelids flutter. The tiny creases at the corners of her eyes are haunting; I can't figure out whether they're from too much smiling or crying.

Sonia opens her eyes and wipes drool from the corner of her mouth with the top of her wrist. She makes a strange noise—a combination of a squeak and groan—and jolts upright.

"Where are we?"

"My house."

"Why?"

"You wanted to come."

Sonia gawks at me as if I'm talking rubbish, then rolls her window down and sniffs at the grassy post-rain air with her eyes closed. She stretches her arms as far as they can go before colliding with the windscreen, and relaxes into her seat again.

"Right," Sonia swallows as if her throat hurts, then frowns. "Where were we tonight?"

I laugh. "Dexter's."

"Oh! Right." She swivels around and looks at the back-seat. "Why are we sitting in the car?"

"Just got here."

"Oh." Sonia laughs under her breath. "I'll shut up now." She grabs her handbag from between her feet, opens the passenger door, and steps out. She clutches at the door handle as if it's the only thing protecting her forehead from the ground.

I get out of the car too. We shut our doors simultaneously, and the sheet metal clunk echoes through the street.

"I've got a question." I scratch my beard. "Why don't you ever invite me over?"

Sonia shrugs and rummages through her handbag. She pulls out an army knife, stares at it, drops it back in, then finds her lipstick. She twists the deep-red-velvet balm through the top of the tube, dabs it on her bottom lip, and then rubs it against her top one. She contorts her mouth to the left as if she were dislodging something from her teeth with her tongue, drops the lipstick back in the bag, and fixes a glare on me as she snaps it shut.

"Perhaps it is . . . dangerous." Sonia laughs with unease.

"Dangerous." I repeat, lowering my chin. "But he's gone."

"It's not that. Mick and I are really messy. You might trip over something, hit your head on the edge of my coffee table, and die." Sonia winks. Her thong scrapes on the concrete.

"Well, clean it. Mia and I are coming over for dinner."

"*Mia* and you? When? I am not sure that is a—"

"Yeah, it is."

We stare at each other, from opposite sides of the car, across the hood. Heat radiates from it like midday sun from a wet road. Sonia purses her lips. "Well. We can make it work, I imagine. But you must tell Mia that Mick will be there. If you leave it to the last minute, all hell will break loose. You know they—"

"I know. I know." I clench and release my jaw.

"Okay. I am just—"

"You told Mick?"

"No."

"Why not?"

"Not sure what I am worried about, really. He will probably just gyrate his hips, make orgasmic sound effects, and—"

I stare at Sonia, expecting her to continue. She stares

back. We both laugh. I'm not sure if it's nervousness or genuine jest. It's been months since we've been in the sack together. Not purposefully. Time flies by without even realizing it. Especially with teenage kids.

I move to Sonia's side of the car and put my arm around her shoulders. I kiss her softly on the nose. With Sonia's head on my shoulder we walk to my front door. Her hair smells like apricots.

As we approach my porch, I notice a heavy thumping and muttering, and fast footsteps on a hard surface, as if someone's doing aerobics. But we have carpet. It doesn't sound like feet on carpet.

I open the door and we step inside. Sonia gasps and brings a hand to her mouth to stunt a laugh. Mia is jogging on the kitchen counter with her arms stretched out from her sides, reciting the lyrics of "White Rabbit" by Jefferson Airplane.

"One pill makes you larger
And one pill makes you small
And the ones that Mother gives you
Don't do anything at all
Go ask Alice
When she's ten feet tall
And if you go chasing rabbits
And you know you're going to fall . . ."

I don't like to swear. I really don't. But what the *fuck*? Mia smiles, not at all put off by us, as she continues to jog and chant the lyrics as if they were pumping her full of air.

"What's going on?" I say, closing the front door behind me with my foot.

"Tell 'em a hookah-smoking caterpillar
Has given you the call to
Call Alice
When she was just small . . ."

I frown and smirk at the same time, rub my hand over my beard, then put my hands in my pockets. I don't know what to do with them. My little-boy instincts make me want to point and squeal. And then I realize this is my daughter. Acting crazy. On my kitchen counter. Singing song lyrics that are more than forty years old.

Sonia looks at me with a huge grin, glances at Mia and back at me again. She points in the direction of my bedroom with her thumb. "I will just—"

I laugh under my breath as Sonia tiptoes out of the room.

But Mia is still jogging. She's going to make herself pass out if I don't get her to stop.

"Mia, get down."

"I'm not finished." She puffs.

"With what?"

"Working out. Burning calories. Getting thin, man!" Mia emphasizes *thin* as if trying to dislodge a parasite from her tongue.

"At two a.m.?"

"I think the question you're looking for, Dad, is 'On the kitchen counter?'"

"That too."

Mia laughs, breathes, laughs, breathes, laughs, and starts to slow down.

"I've been going for about an hour anyway." She sniffs.

"An hour?" I say, with a bit too much shock in my voice.

"I guess. I can stop." Mia levers herself to the ground and squats, balances herself on all fours, and breathes heavily, like she's about to give birth.

I look at my toes, embarrassed—for myself, for her— especially for her. Should I go over to her? Rub her back? Bring her some water? Say something? I dunno what. I'm not good at this stuff. I even get a bit queasy when I see a bloody tampon in the loo bin. I'm a guy. Cut me some slack.

"Do you . . . need anything?" I say, unsure whether I'm s'posed to speak or just let her be.

She shakes her head. Her fringe flicks sweat across her face.

I turn to leave, then turn to face Mia again, step forwards, change my mind, return to my original position. Crikey! I really don't know what the "right" thing to do is. I want to ask her what the hell is going on. She's as high as a bloody kite. Of course she is. But maybe the confrontation can wait until tomorrow. I s'pose that would be the fairest.

"Dad. Just go to bed."

See? I nod. "Okay. You're okay?"

"Yes." Mia groans as if in pain, but I choose to believe it's just annoyance. If I think too much about the stress she's put her body through, I might not be able to resist my overprotective instincts and will rush her to the emergency room. And that would be "embarrassing." So I hold back. She looks like she will be fine after a good sleep. I hope.

"I'm going to bed. See you in the morning?"

Mia nods at the floor, still squatting, and flicks me away like an insect. I leave, shaking my head. I told Sonia something was up. Something *is* up. But is the *something* simply a newfound enthusiasm to get in shape? Could I be reading too much into it?

I open my bedroom door, and Sonia is already under the covers, wearing one of my footy T-shirts, scrunching the doona up to her chest with a cheeky grin on her face.

"What was all *that* about?" she says, as if performing in a pantomime.

I kick off my shoes, undo my belt, and pull down my jeans. I fold them and put them in my drawer where all my jeans go. The shoes I leave in the center of the room, one upside down, the other right-side up. I can handle not putting them outside for one night.

"She's trying to lose weight," I say. I reckon saying it out loud helps me believe it more.

"That looked like a lot more than trying to lose weight."

I cringe. I don't want to hear it. I get into bed with my T-shirt still on. I pull Sonia close. She rubs her thigh against my erection.

"I think she needs a boyfriend," Sonia whispers, and bites my ear.

I laugh and pull the doona over our heads. "You're the one who needs a boyfriend."

"I thought I already had one."

I cup Sonia's left breast in my right hand. "But weren't we just—"

"Not anymore."

"Good. 'Cause I'm getting tired of being the teacher's pet." I wink and slip my hand between Sonia's legs.

Sonia's eyes roll into the back of her head, and she whispers in a really low voice, "Fuck me like I'm dead."

For a split second I want to pull away, but my dick is so hard I ignore my instinct that she's thinking of Ibrahim.

I enter her and she says it again. And again and again, a little more softly each time, until we both come.

After a few moments of catching my breath, I bring it up. "You've never said that before."

"Said what?" she says.

"What you said. About being dead."

"Dead? Who's dead?"

I laugh nervously. "Are you messing with me?"

"No. Why would I mess with you? What are you talking about?"

"You said, uh—" I clear my throat. "Fuck me like I'm dead,"

Sonia glares at me.

"More than once," I add.

Her jaw drops, and a tear escapes the corner of her eye. "I'm sorry. I—I don't remember."

chapter 20

mia

i may look like a cow, but you can go eat
shit if you think you can put me in a
field and bark at me.

Having pulled an all-nighter, I get to school early. I felt totally cool when I left the house, still energetic—less so—but motivated for the day. But the comedown. Man. It's just hit me.

Feels as if I've been injected with the entire world's lack of enthusiasm. My head is full of bees. Buzzing. In slow motion. As if trying to hypnotize me.

Mah he-eh-eh-eh-ed
Is full of beeeeez, yeah.
Bahhhzzing.
In slow moh-shahn.
Hip-no-tah-zing-meee, yeah.

Lyrics. Mental note.
Noted.

I meet Kimi in the corridor by her locker. She's sitting against the wall, legs spread, with her schoolbag between her knees. She's the only one in here, but she raises her hand to get my attention as if amongst a large crowd.

"Hey." I lean my back against the wall and slide my body down into a sitting position with a thud.

"You alright?" Kimi has one eye closed.

I nod and rub my forehead. "I guess." I'm getting a bit of a headache.

Kimi lifts her T-shirt and points to her scar. All dramatic-like.

"*This* is why we've gotta screw this guy over."

And she's just showing me now? I don't get it. This whole strategic let-things-out-one-bit-at-a-time is getting on my nerves. What's the point? She fishing me out? I shuffle my arse backwards a bit to get a better view. Seeing the scar up close, I can tell that the wound must have been pretty deep.

"Shit. That looks painful," I say.

"It was. And I couldn't go to hospital because I—look, that doesn't matter. It's not important. Anyway, I survived. But now he's gotta pay. And that's where you come in. Okay?"

I frown and inspect my nails, thinking that what Kimi just said sounded way practiced and melodramatic. I want to know where this shit is going. What kind of person does she think I am? I'm not gonna go and stab some dude because he stabbed her. But I guess I shouldn't push it until I'm clear about what she wants. And what's with the acting all of a sudden? I used to think first impressions counted. Obviously not. Kimi is not the reserved "mysterious" cool chick I always thought she was. She's . . . well, I don't know what she is yet. I suppose that does make her mysterious. But, you know, not in an intriguing way. Much. I'm sorta getting the feeling that she's as desperate for a friend as I am. So I'm game. I'll let this ride out and see what happens.

"Are you gonna tell me who the guy is?" I say. I tilt my head to the side and notice another scar behind Kimi's ear running along her hairline. It's long and thin and clean.

Cosmetic? Corrective?

"Can't," she says, stretching her arms to her toes, and doing some sort of yoga position.

"How come?"

Kimi sits upright and glares at me as if I'm asking the most ridiculous question ever.

"I think I have the right to know who I'm gonna screw over." I don't mean to snap. It just comes out that way.

"You will," Kimi snaps back. "Eventually. But right now we should just focus on getting you in shape."

The comment stings. What? Is she my personal trainer now?

"Why can't you do this on your own?"

"Are you kidding?" Kimi shrieks, then resorts to a half-whisper. "The guy would kill me. He's too strong."

"What exactly do you need me to do? Why can't you just be honest with me?"

Kimi *tsks*. "I told you I'd tell you soon. I've just gotta figure out a few things. And I need to know you're on my side first. I can't do this on my own. And I can't afford for you to turn on me. Is that honest enough?"

I hardly know you, I think. Kimi stares at me, expectant, eyes like an owl.

"Well? *Are* you on my side?"

This is all too weird. Here we are, sitting in a typical high school corridor, in a typical Melbourne town, living our typical inner-city suburban lives, and all of a sudden we're characters in *Underbelly*? I mean, come on. Get real!

I grit my teeth in frustration. She found my soft spot and pounced. Typical of me to think she was just trying to help. Everyone has an agenda, I guess. Why I thought she was an exception is beyond me. And why did she choose the fat girl? There has to be a reason other than the fact we're both outcasts, doesn't there?

I guess I've been fooled now, and none of that matters anymore. What's important is to take advantage of the free speed and lose weight. If Mum sees me like this, there's no telling what fitness regime she is going to force on me this time. It was hard enough getting over the last one. She had me doing cardio for four hours a day, and I ended up in hospital with heart palpitations. At sixteen, man!

Let's face it. There's nothing stopping me from pulling out of Kimi's plan once I've got my weight under control. Right? And I don't even need to lose it all. Just enough for me to convince my mother that I don't need any help. And if Kimi wants to use me, then I'm gonna use her.

Yeah.

"Yeah." I nod. "I'm on your side."

chapter 21

mick

over me dead fuckin' body

"You fucking sold 'em yet, shit-fer-brains?"

I barely twitch me head to the right as the cunt in the fluoro-green cap and thin greying goatee holds a fuckin' switchblade to me neck. His breath smells like vomit and cat food.

"No? Was that a fucking no?"

I whisper "yes" through me gritted teeth, tryin' not to move me jaw so the knife don't poke into me skin.

"You've got a month. He said if you haven't exchanged 'em for the coke in a month, there are no second chances. But you know what I can't fucking believe, mate?"

I shake me head, take quick breaths through the corner of me mouth, and let 'em out me nose. He's got me locked in his arms, holding me from behind. I can feel his gun stickin' in the crack in me arse, and it makes me want to spit phelgm in his fuckin' face for making me picture the sick cunt butt-fuckin' me in the alley.

"I can't for the *life* of me," he says, drawing out the word *life*, as if tryin' to point out that he has one and I don't, "figure out why he's given you such a long grace period. But I swear, if you do take longer than a month, you know whaddit means, don't you, faggot-shit?"

I close me eyes. I nod. But I swear to fuckin' God, if he lays a fuckin' piss-stinkin' finger on 'er, I won't fuckin' hold back. I'll kill 'im meself. That's a fuckin' promise.

Bile rises in me throat when he spins me round 'n' breathes straight into me face. I wanna dry-retch, but I force it down. I can't let this scum-wanker-cunt think he's got a hold over me emotions. I can't let him know I'm actually shittin' big black motherfuckin' bricks right now. Me own dad. Me *dad* is doing this shit to me. Because he knows how much I love me mum. How much I would do anything to save 'er.

The guy cackles and shows his pointy white teeth with two or three gold ones stuck in there. It sounds like he's runnin' his tonsils over a cheese grater.

"Good," he says, and pushes me backwards. I lose me balance and fall on me arse, whack me head, and pierce me right hand on a rusty nail that's pokin' through a concrete crack. He laughs again, steps a bit further back, and points the switchblade at me from a distance, as if it were a part of his finger.

"One month. I'm not fucking kidding you."

I nod, over and over, gasping for breath through me effort not to cry.

I watch as the guy turns left out of the laneway, only two blocks from me house. He must be bullshittin' me. It's gotta be a test or somethin'.

There's no way me dad would whack me mum. Why now? After all the chances he had of doing it, and gettin' away clean.

I sit up and run me fingers along me neck, to make sure there's no blood. Me heartbeat slows down to somethin' a bit more normal.

Me neck's not cut.

But if I'm not careful, Mum's'll be.

chapter 22

sonia

somewhere over the rainbow

It is seven a.m. and everyone's mailboxes are decorated with dew. When I was a child, I liked to think the dew meant fairies had been out to play during the night. Especially when the sun shone through dispersive prisms of condensation, creating a field of colour across my front lawn. It was the rainbow that first got me interested in mathematics and physics, and its ever-elusive pot of gold. It didn't take long for me to rationalize that the pot of gold was simply the bait to enrich my knowledge.

I hold my ear against my front door, whispering for it to be kind to me today. I am short on time to get ready for school, as I overslept at Nash's house.

A sparrow chirps from the window ledge, as if to tell me the coast is clear, and flutters away.

Quiet. Thank God.

As I twist the key in the front door, I realize Mick forgot to lock it again.

For fuck's sake! I swallow, take a deep breath, and remind myself to stop saying that word. Even when it is only inside my head.

Last time Mick forgot to lock the door, our entire entertainment system was stolen. Along with my iMac, which I had just bought the same week. Since then I have resorted to using my old PC, and failing to collect Mick's weekly monetary contribution for a new computer like he promised. I didn't really expect him to pay me. But the possibility sustained my sanity. He needs focus—some constituent of responsibility. Because God knows his father never taught him more than "be faithful to your brothers."

I open the door, and my heart sinks at the scattered papers all over the floor.

God no. Not again.

I put my bag down and close the door behind me, making sure to be as quiet as possible. Just in case Mick's still here. I cannot bear to face him this morning. Every expression, every wince, every . . . smile, reminds me of Ibrahim. There's no escaping him no matter how much I try. I look around for something other than my stashed pistol to use as a weapon. Nothing. Not even a nail file. The curtain in the lounge room waves about in the breeze.

He's been gone all night? Excellent. Thieves are going to think we're inviting them in!

I sigh and roll my shoulders to try to relax, and notice there is a huge puddle of water on the floor below the windowsill.

I close the window and curtains, drop my belongings on the couch, strip to my underwear as I walk back into the hall, throw my dirty clothes through my bedroom door on the way by, and yank the tea towel with the Periodic

Table on it off the kitchen door handle. And . . . what? The kitchen is *clean*?

I stare at the shiny sink, polished floor, empty dishwasher, while holding the tea towel in the air. A shiver travels down my spine, and I sneeze. It echoes through the whole house, followed by uncertain calm. Goose bumps form all over my naked limbs.

I blink. I must be imagining this. This is not the work of Mick. It cannot be. If it is, is it a sign of progress?

I swivel around on my heel and head back to the lounge room to mop up the water. I kneel on the floor. My knobbly knees dig into the floorboards like chicken bones. I am reminded of scrubbing at the bloodstain on the back porch and the satisfaction I had felt at that moment.

Once I've mopped up all the water, I collect the papers that have flown about the house. Some are supermarket receipts; some are empty envelopes, sealed envelopes, bills, junk mail from Safeway and David Jones. Another blank postcard from Ibrahim. This time from Istanbul. My husband's way of letting me know he's still alive. I feel sick to the stomach every time I receive one. Not because I worry about him. Because he knows I still care. He knows his postcards remind me of our past. He thinks this will bring me back to him. It will not. I have promised myself—and my son—to ignore the temptation.

I single out Mick's offshore bank statement. He black-mailed some banker into opening it for him. Mick apparently had saved him from being busted by the police after handing cash to a hooker. It is who you know, is it not? And of course, there is the whole "be faithful to your brothers." And we know many "brothers."

I stare at the envelope. Thumb already lodged under its corner, ready to rip it open.

Should I?

I do. And I am not at all surprised at the amount of money he has. I was hoping to be surprised at him *not* having any money.

Thirty thousand dollars. At seventeen. With no job. And terrible at maths.

The time has come to call him out on it. It is the only way I am going to fix our relationship. If he knows I know what he is doing, maybe he will have more respect for me. And if I confront him about it, he'll admit it. Because he cannot lie. He can only hide. He is absolutely fine as long as no one asks him about anything. So I will insist that he promise to come clean, return the money to whomever it came from, or I turn him in to the police. Risky, but worth a shot—as long as Ibrahim has nothing to do with it.

Mick's bedroom door is closed. I knock, hold my breath. Just in case. No answer. I twist the silver skull-handle and open the door. A whiff of stale vodka and weed engulf me. I sniff. Cheap sex. And teeny-bopper perfume. My stomach and throat constrict.

Dirty clothes are sprawled all over the floor and bed. Racy panties hang from the light fixture and picture frame hooks. Empty coke bottles, a smashed white saucer, bongs, threads of tobacco on the windowpane that look like furry caterpillars.

I haven't stepped foot in this room for two years. But I cannot play the ignorant and naive mother any longer. Even if I have been doing it for only a short amount of time. If I continue in this fashion, Mick will end up in prison, or worse—following in his father's footsteps.

Mick's wardrobe is open. One side of it is completely empty, bar the one hundred or so manipulated wire coat hangers he has drilled into the wood to create something that looks like a torture chamber. A *seccade*, his Muslim prayer mat, is rolled up in the corner. Does he pray for forgiveness? Did Ibrahim teach him that, too, after I asked him specifically to leave our religion out of his upbringing? My stomach sinks. This is our *son*. And we made him like this.

I take a deep breath. I am in here now, and might as well start looking for something. But is there even anything to find? If his father taught him well, probably not. To be honest, the easiest thing to assume right now would be that he is dealing drugs. But that is stereotypical, and if there is anything I am more certain of, it is that Mick cannot *stand* stereotypical. He has always got to go against the grain. How do I know? I have seen the way he looks at Mia. In the quiet moments in class, when no one is watching. He has a soft spot for her. I know it. I recognize that look. It is straight from Ibrahim's face when we were in high school. It must be in our family's blood. We are attracted to different.

I notice an open cardboard box squeezed between his dresser and the wall. On top is the dark-blue jumper my mother knitted for him when he started high school. I smile, lift it out of the box, and hold it in front of me. The grey light from the window shines through the fabric. I bring the jumper to my nose and sniff.

I miss you.

I imagine it still smells like my mother.

Anise.

I decide to keep it. A token of my son's innocence, a memory of my mother. I close my eyes and whisper, "May Allah bless her soul and make her grave a garden of paradise," out of respect to my parents.

I look at the box again and notice that the whole thing is full of Mick's woollen jumpers. Is he giving them to the Salvation Army? Is he finally getting rid of all his excess junk?

I rummage through the box, to see what he is getting rid of, but as I push some fabric to the side, I hear a heavy muffled thud. So I pull out a couple more jumpers and there are more thuds. They get louder and louder the more jumpers I pull from the box.

I toss the pile of jumpers onto the bed, and reach into the box to pick up one of a dozen or so T-shaped black leather cases. Its weight is quite soothing in my hand, like a stress ball.

I unclip the press stud at the center of the T, hands trembling, heart pulsing in my ears, and slip it from its case.

I am pretty sure I know what it is. But I am hoping I'm wrong.

But I'm not. Push daggers. And they are all engraved with a capital *I*.

I smile . . . until I realize I shouldn't.

chapter 23

mia

maybe he isn't a dickhead after all

I'm supposed to be in Theatre Studies. But I so can't see myself performing that stupid Joan of Arc scenario when I feel so rat shit. I lean against the newly decorated mosaic wall of the auditorium and smoke a ciggie, breathing in slow, long, and hard, the velvety smoke caressing the inside of my throat like a tongue.

I stare across the empty football field at the cluster of old red brick buildings—the English wing—and wonder why Psychology and Advanced Sciences get the new building when English is a compulsory subject. Everybody's got an agenda. Even the people that aren't meant to.

The waist of my jeans digs into my stomach as I bend down to pick up a smooth black oval rock; my dry lips crack as I wince, and my feet burn as gravel scratches the soles of my black baby doll flats.

I slip the rock into my schoolbag. I'll keep it. Maybe I can do something with it in Metalwork. A pendant for Dad maybe. It would be a nice gesture. And I should butter him up a bit anyway, prevent him from finding out about the pills.

The pills. *The Pills.*

I've never done drugs before. What if I get hooked? Caught? What if I lose heaps of weight, but then keep losing it and turn into a freaky anorexic? Ugh. I've seen what that shitty disease does to people. They look like zombies.

Man. Even grosser.

I take another heavy drag of my ciggie, suck my cheeks in as much as possible, and imagine gorgeous cheekbones appearing. But I breathe in too deep and gag and spit yellow foam onto the concrete. As it splatters onto my shoe, someone around the corner of the building kicks something, and yells, "Cunt! Fuckin' stupid fuckin' cunt!"

I drop my cigarette on the ground and with a quick press, twist, and jerk of my heel, I butt it out and lob it under a bench.

There's more swearing, more kicking, more groaning, and I creep to the corner of the building to see what's going on.

It's Mick. Having a tantrum. As usual.

Dickhead.

I roll my eyes and spin around to grab my bag to leave. I can't deal with his shit again. He's a freaking psycho. But just as I hook my arm into a strap, Mick grabs it and yanks me around to face him.

"You spying on me, you fat fuck?" Mick spits on the ground.

A fleck of his saliva lands on my lip. Yuck, gross, ew. I hold my breath and try not to look him in the eye. Instead I focus on a mole by his left nostril. He's got a good grip on my arm; maybe I'm not as fat as I feel. Or maybe Mick's hands are just extra big. I swallow, squint, and channel my own bullying nature back to the surface.

"Nope. You all sooky 'cause your mummy didn't come home last night?" I say.

Mick snarls and inches backwards. He flicks my arm out of his hand like it's burning his palm. He stares at me, arms slightly out to the side as if they are opposing magnets pushing from his torso. He sucks in his top lip and scrapes it over and over with his bottom teeth.

Maybe I should push some more. What have I got to lose? He's gonna try to make my life miserable anyway.

"Didn't Mummy leave you any yum-yums, Mick?"

Mick clenches his fist and lifts it above his head as if about to pound the shit out of me, but he just swings at the air. Man. What a dick.

"What the fuck do you know about that?" he barks.

"About what? Your mother or your dinner?" I scoff, surprised I haven't been smacked or spat at again.

Mick takes a deep breath and closes his eyes. His torso and arms relax, and he squints across the football field; the expression on his face is the epitome of what I was thinking about earlier. Mick hurls a globule of phlegm at the ground and wipes his mouth with the hem of his T-shirt. He looks at me and his nose twitches.

"Can I bum a smoke?" Mick asks, as if trying out a slightly different personality.

I hesitate a little, not sure if I heard right, then fumble through my bag looking for the pack. When I find it, I hold it out in front of me, at a distance, as if Mick were a wild animal that might bite my arm off if I get any closer. He stares at me, then at the pack of ciggies. I glance at my hand, flick the lid open with my thumb. Mick steps forwards, takes a ciggie, launches it into his mouth. He catches it between his lips like a pro and gawks at me. What? Does he want me to congratulate him? I gawk back.

Mick raises his brow in question.

"Uh . . . uh . . . here." I rummage for my lighter. I can't find it.

Mick reaches into his back pocket and pulls one out. Lights his cigarette and blows smoke straight into my face. His lips form a perfect *O*.

I don't flinch.

Mick hovers above me. I'm not gonna let him intimidate me. He's all show. He's got to be. And who would hit a girl? For real? If he did he'd be fucked. My dad would kill him.

"You gonna hang around here all day, pussy shit?" Mick says. Didn't take long for him to stop being "nice."

I scrunch up my nose, numb to the name-calling. "I have as much right to be here as you do, man."

Mick's upper lip twitches. He looks out at the field again and takes another long drag, his ciggie pinched between his forefinger and thumb. When he exhales, he tilts his head and narrows his eyes at me as if scrutinizing every wrinkle that is bound to surface as time goes by.

"You're still hot." He smirks.

I blush and glance in the opposite direction as if I might

have heard someone approaching. I rub my nose, sniff, and look at the concrete, smile a little, hoping Mick can't see it, then draw a star on the ground with my toes.

"Didn't really take you for the type to go for 'Big. Fat. Fucks.'" I laugh. I don't mean to laugh. It just sorta comes out.

Mick cracks his knuckles by pressing his fingers into fists, sits on the bench and rests his elbows on his spread knees. He doesn't ask me to sit, but something makes it seem like an invitation.

So I sit. And place my bag between my feet on the ground.

Mick doesn't look at me, but he smiles and sucks on his ciggie. The tobacco crackles and burns as I watch the smoke slip in and out of his mouth.

I get butterflies in my stomach and gulp.

"The only reason I give ya so much shit," he says, "is because yer the only chick in this school that doesn't break down cryin' every two fuckin' seconds."

I think about the logic of that for a sec. But can't find any. I scoff. "And *how* exactly does that make me a target?"

Mick laughs and shakes his head as if the answer were obvious. "Yourra challenge." He leans closer to my ear and whispers, "I want to *break* you." He glances at me for a split second, grins, and shifts in his seat.

Could he be feeling nervous?

"You're never gonna break me," I say, bumping my right shoulder into Mick's left one. "I'm already broken."

I just touched him. A huge lump rises in my throat, and

my face flushes. I don't know what possessed me to say something so, *so* lame. Mick turns to face me, his smile fading slightly. For a very short moment we hold each other's gaze. Just long enough for me to see another side of him lingering in his eyes.

I grab my schoolbag off the concrete, lay it in my lap, and zip it open. I reach inside and pull out a packet of gum, squeeze a couple of pellets into my mouth, and then offer some to Mick. He shakes his head and rubs his hands over his knees.

"I gotta go." Mick stands, puts his hands in his pockets, and lingers a bit, looking to his left. I look up at him. I want to say something to make him stay. Even if it's something cruel. I don't care. Beats sitting here alone. But I'm too late.

"Take it easy, pussy-shit." Mick winks and disappears behind the building.

I lick my lips as I zip my bag shut and rest it beside me on the bench. I stretch my legs out in front of me and scrutinize my swollen ankles.

Still hot? Man! What's in his ciggies? I chuckle to myself.

I gaze into the sky, shade my face from the sun shining through a gap in the clouds, and smile.

Huh. He actually likes me.

To celebrate, I pop another pill.

chapter 29

nash
just pockets of air

I stare at the e-mail. Clenching my jaw. Wondering why the *fuck* now? Not a word. Not a single word from Celeste. And all of a sudden, she wants to "have a catch-up chat?" On the home phone? Why couldn't she just call in the first place? Why go to the trouble of e-mailing me to say that? We didn't "chat" when we were married.

I scowl at my computer and take a bite out of my nectarine. Juice drips into my beard. I wipe it on my forearm, then my forearm onto my thigh, and jiggle my leg up and down.

Agenda.

I nod at my screen as if it were offering me advice. She's preparing me for something. I know the manipulative drill. How could I forget? Do all women pretend to be nice only when they want something? I haven't noticed Sonia do it. Mia does. But she's a teenager. That's expected.

My shoulders and neck are sore from sleeping pushed up against the wall. Sonia sleeps like a starfish. I stand up and stretch my arms to the ceiling while keeping my eyes on the screen. As if staring at it is somehow going to give me all the answers.

I look around the staff room. It's still early. Empty.

Should be about nine p.m. in LA about now. Should I just get this out of the way and call her myself? Maybe catching her off guard might elicit the real reason she wants to chat. Without cushioning anything. Less time to prepare. Also using the school's phone will save me the cost. There's no way I'm going to tell her to log in to Skype. I reckon she'll stall. Then teachers will start coming in and it will be too late. It's always too late.

I rest my half-eaten nectarine on a serviette and rub my hands on my thighs. I pick up the phone. The cold, light-weight plastic hums in my hand. I break out in a sweat when I bring the receiver to my ear. The dial tone seems louder than usual. I check it's not on speakerphone and dial Celeste's number. Know it by heart from all the times I called and hung up when the separation was fresh.

Karter answers the phone.

"Hi," I croak, and clear my throat. "It's Nash. Is Celeste there?"

Karter groans. "I know who you are. I'd recognize your accent from a hundred miles away."

Likewise, Hitler.

Just as I'm about to reply, something muffles in the phone, as if Karter is pushing the receiver into his chest when he calls for Celeste. I can *just* make out Celeste's fake surprised "Oh?" in the background. Karter is probably glaring at her as if she's going to somehow give me a blow job through the phone.

Tosser.

"Hello, Nash. What a pleasant surprise. How are you?"

I scratch my beard, glance towards the entrance of the staff room to make sure I'm still alone. "Celeste. Don't."

"Hmm, oh, that's fabulous. Yeah, I'm fine, thanks. Is there something I can help you with?"

"I would've thought, after a lifetime of pretending, that you'd do yourself a favour and find someone you could be yourself with," I snap and loosen my jaw. I've just noticed it's clenched.

"I see." Celeste sighs. I can practically hear her lip twitch and nostrils flare.

"Look. What do you want? What was that e-mail all about?"

Silence.

I pick up a biro and stab it into my corkboard. It doesn't go in far enough and drops to my desk with a clack.

"I see. Okay. Well, let me have a think. I could have something prepared for you in a couple of days. Would that work for you? What's your deadline?"

"So you're keeping stuff from Karter as well? I should've fucking known."

Celeste clears her throat. "I'm sorry, I'm not sure I know what you're referring to." Her voice is a little shaky, but probably only enough for me to recognize.

"For fuck's sake, C. Whatever it is, you'd better spit it out. You've caused Mia and me enough grief as it is. What. Do. You. Want?"

"Okay, Nash. That shouldn't be a problem. I'll send you

an e-mail with all the details on how to get started. It's not a complicated procedure."

"No. No, you won't. You tell me what's going on *now*. Figure something out."

Silence.

I bring a fist to my mouth and bite it. This whole thing makes me want to scream. I need a session with the punching bag in the gym.

Fuck.

"I mean it, Celeste," I say through gritted teeth.

Her breath quickens.

"I'll call you back," she whispers and hangs up.

"Fuck!" I bang my fist on the desk. When I look up, Sonia is standing beside me.

"Shit. Sonia. Sorry."

"Not a problem. Sounds like your morning is as bad as mine."

I stand and cup my hands over Sonia's cheeks in an attempt to relax myself. "What's wrong?" I say. A tear rolls down her cheek, and she glances towards the entrance.

"It's Mick. I think he is into something illegal."

"What do you mean? Drugs?"

Sonia gently removes my hands from her face and shakes her head. She swallows, looks at her shoes, and pinches the skin between her eyes.

"Worse. Nash, I think he is selling stolen weapons."

"Guns?" I say a little too loudly, craning my neck.

Sonia frowns and whispers, "No, no—"

My mobile phone rings. I glare at it. Cover my mouth and nose with my right hand and breathe into it like an oxygen mask.

"I have to get this. I'm sorry."

"Should I leave you alone?" Sonia asks with a forgiving yet sad smile on her face.

"Nah. Nah. Here." I roll an absent teacher's seat next to my desk and gesture for Sonia to sit while I pick up the phone.

Sonia sits and pulls a tissue out of her handbag.

"Yeah?" I sigh.

"It's me."

"Alone now?"

"Yes," Celeste says, half whispering. "Barely."

"Get on with it then."

"Okay." It sounds like Celeste is holding her breath.

"Jesus Chri—"

"Mia's not yours."

I glance at Sonia as she blows her nose. "What?"

"She was the result of an assault." Celeste bursts into tears. The sound becomes a little quieter as if she's moved away from the receiver.

"What?" I repeat so quietly I can hardly hear it in my own head.

"I'm sorry. I just couldn't keep it from you anymore. It was burning a hole in my heart. You deserve the truth. Mia deserves the truth."

"You—you—"

"I'm sorry." Celeste blubbers like a child. "Can you not tell her yet? I'd like to visit. I think she should hear it straight from me."

"Excuse me?" I roar, kicking my dustbin. "You can't expect me to—"

"Please!" Celeste wails. "I'm sorry. I've got to—" She hangs up.

I hold the receiver in front of my face. Stare at the beeping plastic like it's an object I've never seen before in my life. Sonia goes quiet and rests her hand on my knee. I turn to face her, swallow a buildup of saliva, dizzy, like I'm being held upside down by my ankles.

"Nash? What's the matter? You have gone really pale."

I drop the phone.

And throw up on the floor.

***

I can't look Sonia in the face. Her eyes are all slanty. Her mouth thin and therapist-like. I hold back the tears. Just. But if I look her in the eye, I'll be a total goner—and a high school parking lot is not the place to lose control of my emotions. Especially since I'm a PE teacher. A *male* PE teacher. And students are storming out of the building like a wild stampede. They'll target my vulnerability as if it's a piece of meat.

I roll two cigarettes on the roof of my car, put one in my mouth, lean my back against the driver's side, and light up. I offer the other one to Sonia with a swift flick of my hand.

Corner eye contact. Glancing at the ground. Gravel. Dark grey. Rock hard with pockets of air.

Just like me.

Sonia looks around her, shifts her weight from foot to foot, shakes her head. I shrug. Put the cig behind my ear.

Usually, I wouldn't let the kids see me smoke. But right now I couldn't give a shit if they saw. As long as I'm not crying and looking like a pussy. Fingers crossed the principal doesn't decide to leave on time today.

"Are you going to be okay?" Sonia half-whispers, resting her hand lightly on my inner elbow. "Is there anything I can do?"

I jerk my arm away. Sonia retracts her hand. I can sense the confusion on her face, but I can't let her touch me. It'll trigger the tears. I *have* to avoid the tears. I sniff and stare in the opposite direction. Sonia swallows, crosses her arms, and looks at the ground. Or her feet. Or the back tyre of my car. I can't tell which.

"Sorry." I face her, but focus on the tiny dark freckle to the left of her mouth. "Not now. Smoke with me?"

I remove the second cigarette from my ear and offer it to her again. Sonia snatches it, purses it between her lips, and leans forwards for me to light it with the end of mine. She shakes her head, stares towards the school gate.

We stand here. In the silence of our synced exhale. Watching the crowd of students leave the school grounds and hoard outside the fish 'n' chip shop across the road.

Sonia slips one hand behind her back and taps her fingers on the car door.

"Are you going to tell her?"

I drop my shoulders, fill my cheeks with air, and let it out slowly with a trickle of smoke. "Should I?"

Sonia pushes her fringe out of her face with the hand holding the cigarette. "I don't know. Do you want to?"

Student voices fill the grounds with ambivalent noise. Car doors open and close, engines roll, gravel grinds as wheels roll towards the comfort of their own homes.

I laugh. Inhale the sweetness of autumn. "What do you reckon?"

Sonia elbows me in the side and juts her chin towards the school gate. I lower my gaze. Mia is approaching with a hippie-looking somebody I have never seen her with before. As far as I can tell, my expression doesn't change.

"Aren't you going to offer her a lift?"

"She doesn't like to ride with me anymore."

"Since when?"

"Couple weeks. Best I don't ask, I reckon."

"Right." The tone in Sonia's voice sounds cynical.

"Please, don't." This time I look her right in the eyes. I can see my reflection, the hazy sun light filling my backdrop like a white sheet.

"I'm not." Sonia looks away. Towards Mia. I look too. The hippie girl starts massaging the back of Mia's neck. They lean against the fence on the outside, and Mia hunches her shoulders as if the massage is too rough, then moves away. The hippy girl puts her hands on her hips. Mia pulls the waist of her pants up and her T-shirt over her hip flab. She yells something, flings her arms around. The silence of that yell from a distance is disconcerting.

Maybe it's just a new friend. A tiff. As simple as that.

"Well—" I open my car door and butt my cigarette out in the ashtray by the gear stick. "I'll head home."

When I reemerge from the car, Sonia is gone.

chapter 25

sonia

$$r = a(1 - \sin \theta)$$

There is a plastic toy truck embedded in my back lawn, disintegrating, slowly sinking from years of weather. Every day for the past fifteen years I have kept reminding myself to dig it up and throw it away. But every day I purposely neglect it.

On the back porch, I stand over the bloodstain, so I can pretend, for a moment, it does not exist. I unfasten the hair clip holding my inarticulate twist together, looking at the truck and the overgrown grass surrounding it, the part I always mow around. The teaspoon wind chime Mick made for me when he was a child preaches melancholic memories in the lukewarm breeze.

Today is the day I let go of the boy and welcome the man—regardless of the man he has become.

I kick off my shoes and cross the lawn to the aluminum shed. Inside, I search for where Ibrahim hid the shovel and gardening gloves. I find the shovel leaning upright against a huge bag of "fertilizer." It's been sealed with staples across the top, but the gloves are nowhere to be seen. Maybe Ibrahim took them. Maybe he is sentimental.

I roll up my shirtsleeves, then spear the shovel into the

dirt surrounding the toy truck, and make four large dents in the earth. In the fourth dent, I pry up the truck just enough for me to jerk it out with my hands. Dirt embeds itself below my nails. I pull hard and almost tumble backwards as it comes loose from my overenthusiastic yank.

I hold the truck out in front of me. The bottom half of it is still bright red and yellow, the wheels clogged with mud. The top part has faded into a pale shade of orange.

Maybe that's all it is. Maybe Mick's just fading on the surface.

"My truck."

I look up at the sound of the fly wire squeaking, still holding the truck in front of me. Mick hovers at the back door. But he won't step onto the porch. He very rarely comes out here anymore.

"Why?" Mick frowns.

I run the truck to the dark-green street bin by the back fence. The snap of the closing lid echoes in my ears.

"Thanks for cleaning the kitchen," I say, brushing off my hands, trying not to touch my clothes. I smile to avoid appearing threatening. I do not want him to think I am going to lecture him about anything. I have done enough of that. And who am I to lecture him about how to behave, anyway?

"I didn't."

"Then who did?"

Mick turns and slams the fly wire door behind him. Something crashes in the kitchen. Pots hitting the floor? Did he just swipe them off the counter?

I have to confront him about the knives. I have to get to the bottom of this, to save my son from his father. For a moment, I think that maybe what he needs is saving from is me. But honestly, if he has gotten himself mixed up with Ibrahim's colleagues, I worry that he will do something "wrong" and get himself killed. I saw what my betrayal did to Ibrahim, the sacrifices he had to make to continue living his life. How he constantly had to run from himself. Could he be back in all his glory, but smuggling weapons instead of drugs under an alias? I would not put it past him.

I return the shovel to the shed and stare at the stapled bag of fertilizer. I suspect it's not actually fertilizer. Do I want to open it and see? I shake my head. My best option is to ignore it. I hardly use anything that is in here anyway. And if Ibrahim is back in town, my bet is the next time I need something from in here, the bag will be gone.

I walk inside. Slam the door. Maybe it is time "Mrs. Shâd" took some time off. Lay off the over-articulation of my speech. Why I thought avoiding contractions made me sound more like a respectable teacher is beyond me.

I pick up the pots from the floor and rest them on the kitchen table. No more pussyfooting around. Time to get dirty.

"Mick! Get the *fuck* out here. Now!"

Mick turns his stereo up full blast.

"I Killed the Prom Queen."

I'd recognize their sound all the way from the Dame Phyllis Frost Centre.

I sit on the edge of the table and bury my head in my hands. Grit my teeth, slam my fists on the table by my thighs. The pots rattle. That's what it sounds like inside my head. Night and day.

I break out in a cold sweat and lick my top lip. Stand. Open the fridge. I eye the slab of steak, but grab a tub of low-fat natural yogurt instead. I peel back the aluminum cover and stare at the gelatinous slush, look at the cutlery drawer, then at the dirty teaspoons in the sink and use one of those instead.

I scoop out a spoonful of yogurt and hold it up to the light streaming through the kitchen window. It's almost translucent. A globule of embryonic membrane. I put it in my mouth. It tastes like snot. I look at the expiry date on the lid. It's two weeks over. I spit the yogurt into the sink, throw the tub in the garbage, cup my hands under the tap to rinse out my mouth.

Violent metal beats and grating vocals rattle something in the hallway.

Roar, roar, roar, roar . . .

I stand in front of Mick's bedroom door and stare at the black Texta marks that conceal the peeling paint. I think of Ibrahim smashing my head against it and feel sick to my stomach. Then the excitement of him penetrating me from behind.

I wipe away a tear and bang on Mick's door. No answer. I try to open it, but it's locked. Anger flushes through my body so fast my veins might burst. I hold my breath, clench my fists, and bang on the door again with both hands.

I scream.

It's so loud inside my own head that my brain vibrates against my skull, and my face feels like it's burning off.

The music stops.

Mick opens the door.

We stare at each other.

My chest moves up and down as I try to catch my breath. Mick doesn't say a word, but a glimmer of pity passes over his eyes.

"Please," I breathe, "we really need—"

"Is this about Mr. Weston?"

I shut my mouth. Blink. Swallow.

"You know about Nash?" I croak.

For a very short moment, the creepiness of Mick's expression makes me forget he's my son, and I feel violated.

"Don't get yer scanties inna knot. I don't give a fuck." Mick picks at a bit of paint from the door frame, peels it off, rolls it into a ball, and flicks it over my shoulder.

I squint. Wish he'd do something about those blackheads. What a stupid thought to have right now. But maybe it's the mundane things like this that I can rely on to prevent me from retreating into my prior self.

Mick glares back. "Whatcha think? I'm gonna crack the shits 'cause he's not Dad?"

I look down the hall as if I've heard a noise. I haven't. But I need to look away. Mick's eyes haunt me. I wonder if he notices. If he cares. "No, I—"

"Dad is a *cunt*. The homeless dude down the road could look after us better."

"Oh. Well—"

"Yeah, go 'head. Have 'em over. Fuckin' A. I promise I won't spit in Mia's face."

Mick slams the door in my face and turns his stereo back on. The heavy metal razors cut through the walls, my head, and my heart.

I kneel on the floor to relieve the sudden dizziness and notice a faint footprint near the front door, but it doesn't look like it's from Mick's runners. I crawl over to take a closer look.

Army boot.

Ibrahim.

I hold my breath. I knew it.

He never left.

flash-forward

A small gasp. Female.

"What happened? What's going on?"

A man coughs, spits on the road—it splatters like phlegm. He tells the woman to shut the fuck up.

"Oh my God, I can't feel my legs. I can't feel my legs!" she cries.

"Don't move, ya cunt—stay in the fuckin' car." The man's voice quivers, its tone anxious, familiar. I think I know who it is. But it can't be.

I roll onto my side, clenching my teeth through the sharp stabbing in my leg, and look towards the voices. It's Mum, face covered in blood, trapped in a rent-a-car wrapped around a tree. What is she doing here? Why?

My breath quickens. I look at the car, and at Dad, still motionless. Shooting pain crawls up my left arm and into my neck like an electric shock.

I look up. It is him.

And he has a knife to Mum's throat.

chapter 26

sonia

cytotoxic lymphocyte

The kettle boils. Its auto-stop is broken. I neglect to switch it off. Instead, I remain seated at the kitchen table, staring at the steam hitting the base of the cupboard above it, watching condensation form on the cream gloss finish, listening to the whistle become fiercer and fiercer, until the water bubbles through the nozzle and splashes on the counter, an inch from my mobile phone.

I remember the time Ibrahim held my head over this steaming kettle. It lasted for only a brief moment. If it wasn't for the steak knife resting on the counter from the previous night's meal, I wouldn't have walked away with anything less than third-degree burns covering the right side of my face. Sometimes I wonder whether physical scars would have been better than the emotional ones it left behind. I stabbed him just below the ribs. It was shallow. But I haven't had a decent night's sleep since. Mainly because I enjoyed it so much. Someone needs to put me down. I don't know how much longer I can keep this up.

I stand. Switch the kettle off from the power point on the wall.

I flip open my mobile and lean my hip against the counter.

Message Nash.

I'm sorry I ditched you in the car park. I was upset about what I found in Mick's room. I was upset that you didn't seem to care. Can you forgive me? BTW, I told Mick about us, and he thinks it's great. So let's all do dinner?

I stare at it. Bite the inside of my left cheek. Delete it and start again.

I told Mick. Dinner is a go. PS: I'm sorry.

I groan. Delete it again.

Told him.

I press Send. Flick the phone closed. Wait.

I shift the weight between my feet, rest the mobile on the counter, and watch it until the screen dims.

The phone vibrates, flashes blue. I flip it open again, open the message.

great

I take a deep breath and slowly exhale through my nose. I want to leave it at that. To not give Nash the impression that I need him to stay sane, to stay . . . clean. But can't help myself.

Sorry about today.

OK

What night?

Talk tomorrow.

I want to call him. The messages are unsatisfying. I have to make sure he's okay. No. Make sure he's okay with *me*. But I don't. I resist. If I call, it will only make me feel worse— unwanted. He's obviously in a rotten mood. And I don't blame him. What an awful thing to find out about Mia. Celeste was so lovely in high school. She took me under her wing, helped me become "cool." She even convinced me to hook up with Ibrahim so I could become a more solid member of their group. She used to be so down-to-earth. I wonder what turned her into such a fitness-and-beauty freak? And what kind of mother leaves her only child with a man she suspects isn't the biological father? It just doesn't make sense.

I turn my phone off and head to bed, feeling like all the colour has drained from my skin and into my childhood rainbow. I think about Mick's prayer mat and contemplate pulling it out. Maybe I need to reunite myself with Allah. Maybe he can help me continue to be a good mother, to keep suppressing my older self, the craving to sin. But I can't stop likening the prayer mat to a pool of blood. And that just makes me lose touch with reality even more.

Because the last time I prayed was over ten years ago.

The day I was baptized a killer on our back porch.

chapter 27

nash

is. and always will be.

I lie on my back. On the grass. By the Yarra River. Smoking. Contributing to the grey of the low-hung clouds. I don't want to go home. How can I look Mia in the eye and keep Celeste's secret? And for fuck's sake, I don't give a shit whose junk conceived her—she's still my daughter.

My daughter.

Always will be.

But will Mia feel that way? What if the mere technicality of it sends her spiraling into an even bigger depression? What if she goes to live with Celeste in LA? How would I cope? The thought of losing the only person I love more than I loved footy is hard to swallow.

Assault? That is rich. Really rich, Celeste.

Leaves rustle in the wind. A cyclist's chains clink as they glide by my head only a metre from the footpath. Cars rumble on the bridge behind me. The sun disappears, thunder cracks, and rain pelts down.

But I don't move.

I close my eyes, allow myself to become as soggy as my cigarette. I throw it towards the river knowing it won't even make it close. This time I don't feel guilty. The river is brown. City brown shit pollution crap, what-the-fuck-are-we-doing-wrong *brown*.

What's one more fag?

What's one more sorry broken soul taking his shit out on the river?

What difference does it make?

"What difference does it fucking make?" I roar, punching both fists and feet repeatedly towards the sky.

And then it finally happens with one huge breath of wet air.

I cry.

I cry, and my body trembles against the earth.

chapter 28

mia

lost in a labyrinth

I pop another pill, sit cross-legged in the middle of my bedroom floor, categorizing the music on my iPod: male, androgynous, goddess. My left knee bounces up and down, the fat of my calf acting as an air bag. I press play on "Bird Song" by Lene Lovich in the "goddess" category and look at my window. It's raining. The drops splatter on the glass like giant spitballs. All I want to do is jump. On a trampoline. I regret letting my dad throw it away.

Trampoline in the rain, trampoline in the rain, Hi-Ho the Derry-O, trampoline in the rain . . .

The phone rings, shrill in my left ear as I adjust my earphones, a mix between tweeting birds and nails down a blackboard. But I dance to my feet anyway, trying on the dub step moves, unsuccessfully, but who cares. Man, at the moment I feel like I could do anything.

I yank the earphones from my ears and drop my iPod on the bed, dance to the living room, answer the phone; the smile on my face fades when I hear her voice.

"Mia? Darling?"

"Oh. Mum."

"How are you?"

I look at my reflection in the picture frame on the wall, my face an essence within a nostalgic footy game, Dad in the motions of kicking the ball towards the goalposts, his mouth contorted with passion—young, handsome, pre-single father lost in the labyrinth of responsibility.

"Same," I say quietly.

Lahhhst in a laaabrynth . . .

"How's your— How's Nash?"

I shrug. "Same."

Lahhhst in a laaabrynth . . .

Silence. Saliva. Scent of suppressed hunger.

Kids screaming, running in the street in the rain—it filters through the open window. I want to join them. Play hopscotch, clapping rhymes, grow up . . . nicer.

"Ah. . . how's—"

"Why are you calling?" A dog barks and growls. Next-door neighbour tells it to move, it whimpers, a door slams shut.

Mum laughs. Squeaky. Phoney. Small.

"Sweetie, I'm just calling to see how you are."

Singsongy.

Lahhhst in a laaabrynth . . .

"You never call just to see how I am."

Mum inhales. Drama queen. I picture her nostrils flaring and bite dry skin off my top lip. Something pings through the phone. A microwave maybe. Or maybe Karter gave her a time limit on the phone, and this is her cue to get off. Wouldn't be fucking surprised. Arse.

"So. I did have a reason for calling actually. I just wanted to let you know that I'm coming to visit! Good news, isn't it?"

I hold my breath and look at my swollen ankles, my wrists, the ring I can't remove from my middle finger. My cheeks flush—an urgent need to run, to run anywhere—pinches just below the surface of my skin like an itch, an itch, the creepy crawlies in my bones, eyes hot, they sting, like I need some water, I've been forgetting the water, forgetting to eat, when did I eat, when did I stop thinking about the chocolate under my bed, oh shit, oh shit, oh fuck, visit? What? When when when?

"When?" I ask.

"Oh. I was thinking . . . around a month?"

I shriek, "A month?"

"A month isn't good? What's happening? You going away or something? I don't want to intrude, just let me know when it's a good time, the last thing I want to do is—"

"No! No, it's fine, I mean, I was just . . . just surprised. Happy surprised, you know. I . . . er . . . I miss you." I roll my eyes. What am I going to do? How am I going to lose all this weight in only one month? I can't let her see me like this.

"Oh, that's a relief. For a moment there I thought you didn't want me to see you."

I choose not to answer that. "Is, uh, Karter coming too?"

"No." Mum scoffs under her breath.

I nod. The receiver sweats in my hand, I grip it tighter; I

want to strangle it. The voices outside, the kids' voices, they seem louder—are they coming over? Do they want to play? Has it stopped raining? There's no noise, it's just a hum, a thick hum around my head, creeping up my nose, sleeping on my eyelashes, hammocks to the sound waves.

Sleeeeepang on mah ahhhlashes . . .

"I'll bring you some really nice designer outfits. How's that sound? You're still the same size, aren't you?"

I close my eyes. Hold my breath, try to hum this feeling down to my feet and into the floor and into the earth and into the core. The darkness behind my eyes transforms into coloured swirls, and for a moment I feel like I'm floating. Is it relief? Am I falling asleep? Standing?

"Mia? Are you there?"

I flick my eyes open and touch the flab under my chin.

"I, uh, yeah. I'm still the same size." I lower myself to the floor and hug my knees. I look between my legs, at the way my stomach folds over itself.

I'll be the same size.

"Fabulous! I have the perfect outfit for you. Fun! Are you excited?"

I smile at a thin image of myself. I'll never do this on time. Maybe I should leave town, quit school. Nothing here for me anyway. Go somewhere where no one knows me, hide out for a while until I'm back to my normal size, then return, you know, all happy and shit, and say, surprise, I'm not actually dead, man. I'm sorry I made you cry.

"Yeah. Full-on excited," I say, rolling my eyes again. Funny how I sound so convincing.

Mum claps. "Let Nash know, okay? I haven't had a chance to speak to him."

"Okay."

"Fabulous. Speak soon?"

"Sure."

I return the receiver to its hub, and Dad opens the front door, sopping wet, pale, shivering, gasping for breath.

"Dad, you have to tell her no!" I cry, standing up too fast, feeling dizzy and balancing myself against the wall.

Dad lifts his cap, smoothes his hair into it, and puts it back on. He shakes his head, grabs a T-shirt off the arm of the couch, and wipes his face dry. "What are you on about?"

"Mum. She said she's coming over. In a month!"

"Oh."

"Oh? Look at me, Dad. I'm a fucking rhinoceros."

"Mia, she's not going to care."

"Of course she'll care," I scream, tears streaming down my cheeks. "Look at who she married."

"Mia—" Dad steps towards me, reaches for my shoulders.

"Don't touch me. I should have known. Why would you care what Mum thinks of me? You probably agree with her. You think I'm a fucking fat ugly bitch just like everybody else. No wonder you keep pushing me to lose weight. You can't stand the sight of me, can you?"

"Mia, it's not like that. I'm just concerned about your health. Please, can you—"

"No. Leave me the fuck alone." I grab the picture frame off the wall, of Dad playing footy, and hurl it across the room. It shatters on the TV and screams *I hate you*.

I stare at Dad, I want to say "sorry," I want to take it back. Dad has tears in his eyes, *tears*, he never cries. I've never seen him cry.

I run into my bedroom, sobbing, choking on my own thick breaths, wishing the big fat ugly bitch in me would just die, die, die.

I rummage through my schoolbag and pull out the plastic Ziploc of pills. I empty it onto my bed.

There are only two left.

I swallow them both and clench my jaw until my head hurts.

I'm so fat I probably can't even overdose.

I grab my iPod, put the earphones back in. Go for the goddess. Today's goddess. I press Play, stand still, straight and tall, pretending to watch myself from above.

Courtney Love.

Skinny Little Bitch.

chapter 29

nash

i think i've lost her anyway

I pick up the photo and the glassless frame off the floor, focus on Ibrahim, his pouted mouth and stocky legs. I rest the photo on the arm of the couch. Coach Warren gave it to me. A gift. A message. A sign I'd be the one to "make it."

Yeah, I miss my footy days. I even miss the kinds of matches when it pelted down with rain. Once, it was raining so hard I couldn't see properly, and I slammed into a fellow team player when we both jumped to catch the footy midair. I broke my collarbone. He fucked up his nose. We were mates. We shook hands and laughed about it. *That* was brotherhood. Not the team of psychos Ibrahim assembled when I married Celeste.

So? I could have become a pro player. Could have won trophies. But you know what? Mia is my trophy. And the only trophy I'll ever need. Maybe I didn't make it to the AFL, but I made it somewhere. And this place? It's so much more special than a career that would probably have lasted a decade, if that.

The fact that I "made it" as Mia's father is enough.

I can't lose her.

I just can't.

I go to the laundry; grab a plastic bin bag, the brush, and pan; return to the living room and scoop up the shards of glass. They hit the bottom of the plastic bag like I-told-you-sos. I leave the bag by the front door for the next time I go out.

In the kitchen, I open the fridge, grab myself a light Carlton Draught, and contemplate ordering some takeout. Vegetarian pizza maybe. But what about Mia? She shouldn't be eating that stuff—even the garden variety. I've gotta be strong for her. I've gotta be strict, even if she hates my guts and lashes out. So what? I'll be her punching bag. Crikey, that's what parents are for.

I stare at the blank chunky '90s TV screen, swig my beer, listen to the rain stop and start like God's got prostate cancer. I switch the TV on for some background noise. I need to change clothes, but I head to Mia's bedroom first, my wet footsteps as heavy as my heart.

I knock on her door.

No answer.

I knock again. Call her name. Jiggle the handle. Call her name.

Do I force it open? Or leave her alone? I have to confront her about her behaviour before she damages herself.

There's movement, sound, like beads moving around a glass bowl, her wardrobe door swinging shut, a rustle of clothing, humming. As I reach for the handle again, the door swings open. Mia is lip-syncing, earphones in. Thick black shadow lines her eyes; her mouth is glossed red like fresh blood. Mia tries to push past. I block her, gripping the frame of the door on each side.

"Take them out," I say, jutting my chin towards her earphones. Mia stares at my mouth; the corner of hers turns up. She raises her brow as if to say "fuck off," jittering with an urgency I have never seen before.

"Please," I mouth.

Mia clenches her jaw; looks at my left hand; whacks it down with both her arms, buckling my elbow; and slips past me. I grab her by the back of her T-shirt, pull her so hard it looks like she's about to choke from the collar tight around her neck. I spin her around to face me. She gasps, eyes open wide. I breathe into her face, holding both her shoulders taut, yank her earphones out, and push her into the wall, just hard enough for her to know I mean business.

"What's going on? Tell me now."

"Piss off." Mia spits in my face. I can't believe it. I back up, glare at her, wipe her spit off with the hem of my wet T-shirt.

Mia glances towards the front door, at my chest, then at the floor. "Fuck. I'm sorry. I . . . I shouldn't have—"

I flare my nostrils and put my hands in my pockets, open my mouth to speak, but nothing comes out. I want to yell and scream and shake the shit out of Mia, tell her to show me some respect, but I don't. It'll only make things worse. Plus, she just apologized. Even if it was motivated by a threat of not being let out of the house, she still did it. That says something. I should let it slide. Get to the bottom of what really matters here.

"Where you going?" I say on the exhale.

"Out."

"Where out?"

"Just a friend's house."

"It's a school night."

Mia shrugs. "Maybe we'll study."

I shake my head. Mia's eyes are glazed. Reflecting the shame I feel for all the crap I let Celeste put us through. We were a family. A happy one. Then all of a sudden Celeste decides we're not good enough for her and runs off with a rich prick who treats her like a rich prick's wife. What was she thinking? And now? Why? What's the point of telling me now? Is this a part of some scheme to try to get custody of Mia?

Mia glares at me, flushing saliva back and forwards between her front teeth. She seems high. I scratch my beard, lean my back against the opposite wall and look at the floor.

I need to think.

"Can I go now?" Mia says with a fake smile.

I've just gotta ask her. Straight. "You on something?"

"What? No." Her overly shocked expression tells me she's lying. But I will give her a chance to come clean.

"Just tell me. I won't be upset. I just wanna help you."

Mia brushes hair out of her face and adjusts her T-shirt. "Don't be stupid."

"You think I'm being stupid?"

"Yeah. It's a stupid question."

"I'm not blind. Explain the—"

"Man! It's not 'cause I'm taking drugs. I'm dieting. And it's hard. And it's driving me fucking nuts." Mia clutches her head, actions to demonstrate her explanation, I s'pose. Does she really think I'm that stupid? As if I need visuals to help me understand. "I need to, uh, keep busy, uh, to stop thinking about it." Mia looks me right in the eye and stops fidgeting for a moment. It seems like it's taking a lot of effort and concentration on her part to stand still. "That's all. That's all it is. I promise."

I look towards the front door and press my lips together. She's convincing. But I can see it in her eyes that she's on something. How far do I push? How far can I interrogate her without pushing her to leave home? That's what Celeste and I did as soon as our parents started questioning our behaviour. We thought we were invincible. We thought our parents were old-fashioned, overprotective, and over-reacting. We thought that life would be easier on our own, without the hassle of listening to their lectures about drugs and contraception. Is that how Mia feels right now? Is this conversation the beginning of me pushing her out of my life?

I'll let it go. For now.

"You still need to eat, mate," I say. "What have you eaten today?"

Mia rolls her eyes. "Fruit. A salad."

"When? Lunch?"

Mia nods.

"Dinner?"

She shakes her head.

I sigh, groan under my breath, yank my wallet out of my back pocket, and slide a twenty-dollar note out. "Promise me you'll get something to eat on the way."

Mia nods again, grabs the twenty, puts it in her back pocket, looks at her feet while clicking her tongue as if to say "Can I fucking go now?"

I cross my arms. Mia walks to the front door, puts an earphone in, pauses, spins around to face me, and smiles.

"Her name's Kimiko. Kimi for short." Mia's top lip twitches. "You'd like her."

I nod and watch Mia close the front door behind her.

The house fills with a suffocating invisible fog. I remove my cap and my wet T-shirt, run my fingers through my damp hair. I roll the T-shirt into a ball and hurl it at the door. It hits with a thick slap and flops to the floor.

And I have a terrible feeling, that this day has marked the beginning of our end.

chapter 30

mia

no one is ever what they seem

I stand outside Kimi's house, wondering whether I have the right street, right house number. I look at the directions on my phone again. Look at the house.

This is it. I am repulsed.

It's a fucking two-storey mansion. White, blinding, even in the dark. Floor-to-ceiling windows deck the entire left side, which faces a block of land filled with trees. The lights are all off except a smallish circular one on the far right of the second floor.

I text Kimi to tell her I'm here, like she told me to. My hands are trembling, and I keep making stupid typos, biting my tongue in frustration at the auto-correct.

I rub out the text five times before I get it right. Almost: *I'm outsider.*

I send it anyway. My stomach gurgles. The insides of my legs feel like they're filling with soda. I grit my teeth, flex my toes, clench my fists.

I need . . . more.

Something creaks behind me and I spin around. I think I see a shadow of translucence, like a jellyfish floating by. My nose is itchy. I rub it. Squeeze it. Sniff. Wipe it along my wrist.

Kimi slowly opens the front door and holds her finger to her mouth. Gestures for me to tiptoe in. Kimi takes me straight up to her bedroom without even introducing me to her parents.

Everything is white, black, and chrome. Everything. Art Deco–like. A mini retro hospital. Kimi is even wearing a grey tracksuit with freaking diamantes arranged in the shape of a heart on her left bum cheek. Kimi gestures for me to slip off my baby doll flats.

They're flats, you idiot, I think.

I stare at Kimi's arse as she leads me up the spiral staircase. *Bumshell.* I giggle.

Kimi turns around and *shooshes* me with a frown.

The first thing I see in Kimi's room is my reflection in the mirror directly opposite the door. I look and feel like a piece of stale toast crust.

Kimi closes the door, rolls her eyes, groans, and falls backwards, arms out to her sides, onto her king-sized bed with white lace frills bordering the bottom edges of the mattress.

"They're not my real parents," Kimi mumbles.

"What?" I stand in the middle of the room, wondering where to sit, afraid I might stain something with my inferiority.

"I'm adopted." Kimi sits up, crosses her legs under her sparkly butt, and flings her arms in the air. "Can't you tell?" She laughs, but I don't get the joke.

I chuckle, not sure whether to feel pity or pleasure towards Kimi resenting good fortune. "Does your mum dress you too, then?"

Kimi glares at me, clearly not impressed by my sarcasm.

"Sorry." I drop my bag and flats on the floor and look at my toes. I need to cut my nails. "I'm all out," I say, and look up again.

"Already?"

I shrug, trying not to blink a hundred times a second, trying not think about pissing all over Kimi's fluffy white carpet. I need the loo. *Badly*. "I took the last two before I came." I glance at Kimi to see if she freaks out. *I* am kinda freaking out. What if something happens to me after taking two pills at once? My limbs already feel floaty.

Kimi smiles as if she's got a secret. "Chill out. You should see the look on your face." She bursts out laughing again.

I swallow, walk to Kimi's state-of-the-art dresser, open the top drawer to see what's in it. These drugs make me do weird shit. I would never even think to pry like this normally. And I'm doing it so casually, without a care. And I don't care. I just "am." Like my existence is a gift to the world. And whatever I do in it is inconsequential.

"What the fuck are you doing?" Kimi says.

I click my tongue. "Getting to know you."

Kimi jumps up, pushes in front of me, and flicks the drawer closed with her knuckles before I see beyond the abundant collection of nail polish arranged perfectly by shade. The drawer rolls and snaps shut.

"Nothing in there that's gonna help you, chickie."

"Chickie?" I laugh. "Who *are* you?"

"No one is how they seem."

I raise my eyebrows and let out a big breath. "I don't even know why I'm here."

"I do," Kimi says.

I narrow my eyes at her. Her sly smile is so slanted, I'm amazed her mouth isn't sliding off her face.

"So, let me get this straight. You're just using me to sort out this stupid revenge thing you're going on about. And you think getting me addicted to speed is going to keep me in your company and eating out of your hand?" I laugh—actually, I think it's more of a cackle—trying to ignore the pulsating in my temples and the sweat accumulating on my top lip. "As if."

Kimi shrugs. "Well, it worked, didn't it? You're here trying to score."

"Can I just ask you one more time?" I say. "Why me? I mean, why not miss-piss-my-pants-in-Ping-Pong, who never learned to say no?"

Kimi looks at the ceiling, dramatizing her reaction with a contorted mouth and a scratch of her head. "You seemed, uh, let's see . . . more vulnerable?"

I knew it. Great. So it's obvious to everyone. "I'm not vulnerable," I say. Seriously? I don't even believe that myself, so why would she?

"Not anymore. You've got the drugs to thank for that."

"You're a fucking bitch." I don't know why that just came out of my mouth, but a sense of power is surging through me that makes me think of vampire poison flushing through my veins.

"So are you."

Why is Kimi acting so calm? Does she really think she's all that?

I crane my neck and drop my jaw. "*You* manipulated *me*. How does that make me a bitch?"

"You can't remember a thing, can you, Mia?"

"Remember a fucking thing of what?" I wipe the sweat from my lip with the top of my wrist and cross my arms in one smooth transition.

"That day you burned my clothes in PE."

I suck my tongue to the roof of my mouth.

That was . . . her?

"Shit." My arms fall to my sides and Kimi inches closer, practically blocking me into a corner.

"Yeah. Shit."

"Uh . . . you looked so different then."

Kimi scoffs, shrugs, pulls out another little Ziploc bag of pills from her bra. She holds it out for me between two fingers. "So did you."

I look at the pills, feeling like my eyes are crossing to gain focus. I contemplate turning them down, getting out of this little grave Kimi seems to be digging for me. I'm not myself. I know this.

These drugs. These drugs, they're bad for me. But it's so *cool*. This feeling. Of control. I feel alive and free and floaty, and I love and hate everyone at the same time. Maybe I don't even know which feeling is which. Maybe it's indifference. But I don't care. And I don't care about my weight so much, either. And I've already lost two kilos. Maybe this is what they call freedom. But I'm not stupid. I know they're beginning to screw with my head. I mean. Fuck. I spat in Dad's face. I would never have even considered doing that if I wasn't high. I didn't even think about it; I just did it. Like a reflex. I know I should stop taking these. I *know*. I will stop. Just one more round, and then I will stop.

I promise. It's an honest-to-God promise.

I snatch them out of Kimi's hand and put them in my pocket, hoping I don't regret this.

Kimi grins. "Would be nice if you could contribute a little cash for—"

"I'm trying to figure out why I'm okay with you manipulating me," I say, turn ninety degrees to face the dresser mirror, and wipe a small smudge of black from my right cheek. On top of the dresser is a picture of Kimi and some older guy. Really dark-skinned. The guy looks familiar, but *who* isn't quite registering. It's probably her adopted father.

Kimi puts her hands around my waist from behind and rests her chin on my shoulder. We look into each other's reflected eyes in the mirror.

"I'm not manipulating you," she says. "It's a simple case of I scratch your back and you scratch mine. And there's more to you. I'm curious. You're interesting." Kimi lowers the tone in her voice to a featheriness that reeks of sexual innuendo.

I purse my lips and turn around to face her. Kimi pushes her boney pelvis against my robust hip, hooks my hair behind my ears, and whispers, "You're not afraid of me, are you?"

My stomach tightens and tingles travel down to my crotch. Kimi's lips move closer to mine; she smells like white musk. Saliva accumulates under my tongue, but all I can think about is Mick being here too. If he was, I wouldn't pull away.

Just before Kimi's lips touch mine, I swivel my head to the right. I can't do this. I want to try it. But I can't. It just feels wrong. Kimi steps backwards and gives me room to move away from the dresser and stares at the floor with her arms crossed.

I grab my bag, hook it over my shoulder, and pick up my flats.

"You really should tell me what it is you need me to do." I say, and stand by the door. "You can't bait me with speed forever, man. At some point I'm not gonna want it."

"I don't need to tell you anything. You can easily help me on the spur of the moment. It's not as if I need you to plan a murder. I just want you to—" Kimi holds her forehead like she has a headache. "You're just going do something in a place I can't be seen. That's all."

"That's all? This is stupid. Why can't you just tell me?"

"I'm trying to protect you. If I tell you, you might be liable."

"Liable? For what?" This doesn't sound good.

Kimi flicks her head towards the door. "I think you should go now."

"Why?" Is she serious?

"You just should. My foster father doesn't know you're here, and he'll be up here to check on me any minute."

"But—"

"You got what you came for, didn't you?"

She shuffles me to the front door. "Sorry. I'll see you tomorrow." Kimi smiles as if she's a little embarrassed. Maybe she's really in trouble and genuinely needs my help. Maybe I'm being too suspicious. Maybe I'm just a clueless idiot.

I open my mouth to say "okay," but Kimi closes the door on me before I can even utter the "O."

I stare at the chrome knocker, imagining the taste of musk in Kimi's mouth. I've never been attracted to a girl before, and I wonder if it's the influence of the speed or the effects of being "needed" for something, even if I am being totally taken advantage of.

I turn around and walk out through the front gate, wondering where I'm going to go that's not home, when I think . . . *foster* father? She said she was adopted when I arrived. Is she full of total shit, or what?

I feel inside my back pocket. The twenty-dollar bill Dad gave me for food is gone. Did Kimi pickpocket me? I backtrack through the events in her bedroom, trying to pinpoint the exact moment she grabbed it, and I suddenly realize where I've seen that dark-skinned guy before.

He was in that footy photo with Dad.

The one I smashed against the wall.

I pop three Xanax and swallow them without any water.

chapter 31

celeste

no more botox

My throat stings as I breathe in the metallic air of Karter's office, and I clutch his door handle in an attempt to stop my hand from shaking. Karter's secretary, Freda, hovers behind me, whispering for me to reconsider interrupting him right now: He's *very* busy.

And we all know what that means, don't we?

I flick Freda away like she's filth.

I close my eyes, take a deep breath, and exhale as I twist the handle and swing the door open. Karter's head is down, a tuft of hair reaching for the ceiling, red pen in hand, scribbling with abandon on what seems to be some sort of report. A woman in a black leather skirt is sitting cross-legged on his sofa, buttoning up her white blouse. She winks, smirks, grabs her leather jacket off the armrest, and shrugs it on.

"Darling," Karter says, still scribbling. He doesn't look up. "As you can see, I'm slightly busy at the moment. Make an appointment with Freda. I think I have a cancellation this afternoon that I can slot you into."

Sofa Woman stands, licks her lips, and says, "Ich hätte meine Muschi lieber dir überlassen."

Freda gasps.

Karter stops scribbling, looks up, and smiles at me. Little does he know that I learned German in high school and can pretty much figure out what she said. Repulsed, but slightly flattered by her lesbian advance, I scoff at Sofa Woman as she brushes against my shoulder on the way out.

"Very well." Karter nods at Freda hovering behind me in the doorway. "Freda, you may leave Celeste here with me. It's fine."

"Yes sir." Freda nods and closes the door.

I run my tongue along my teeth and hug my handbag to my chest. The room smells like a barber shop. Was he shaving in here? Oh . . . her pubic hair. What a laugh! He did that to me before our very first sexual encounter at the Hilton in Melbourne. He hit on me at the bar. I was supposed to meet Ibrahim for a drink. But his stupid wife decided to get arrested that night, and he didn't want to risk being seen in public.

"What is it you want?" Karter laughs. "Change your mind about the Botox?"

"I wouldn't let you stick me with another syringe if my life depended on it," I snap.

Karter caps his pen and aligns it next to a pile of papers. He cups his hands together and rests them in front of him. "I see. What is it you want then, dear?"

"A divorce."

Karter scoffs, props up his feet on the corner of his desk, and runs his fingers through his hair. "That might be difficult at this point in time. I have a lot on my plate."

"I'll take care of it." My voice quivers as I force myself to relax my limbs before I snap in half. "I'll have my lawyer send you the documents. From today, you will communicate with me through my lawyer only. I'll have him send you all the necessary documents to—"

Karter sits upright and smacks his hands on the desk. "Back up a minute. You can't just—"

"Of course I can." I snicker. "And don't worry. It will be done quietly. The press won't hear a peep of it until your grant is awarded."

Karter clears his throat. "And what, may I ask, did I do to deserve your discretion?"

"Nothing. It's what you *will* do. And if you don't do it, you know exactly who I can ask to pay you a visit." Ibrahim and I have stayed in touch.

"I see." Karter laughs again as he gets out of his seat, walks around his desk, and sits on its front edge. "How much is this going to cost me?" He crosses his arms and narrows his eyes like he's trying to read my mind.

I swallow, hold my breath, and let it all blurt out. "I want a million dollars, a ticket to Australia—for as soon as possible—and for you to never, *ever*, contact me again."

Karter nods and stands. He holds his fingers to his lips in thought. What a parody.

"I'll give you two million if you remain at my beck and call until the spotlight fades."

"I refuse to stay."

"Then I suppose I misjudged your needs."

Now he's getting cocky. "What do you mean by that?"

"We had an unspoken agreement, did we not?"

I clench my teeth. I knew threatening him with Ibrahim wasn't going to work. He has his own connections that could do Ibrahim and his family just as much damage. I can't even imagine Ibrahim being any sort of saviour anyway. He loves his stupid wife too much. But I have just the thing to counteract it.

"Wasn't I your so-called shield of protection? From your less-than-favourable past? Isn't there something you wish to keep from your imbecile of an ex-husband? Not to mention the fact that such news, I imagine, would be absolutely devastating to your daughter."

I step closer to Karter with more conviction than I've ever had in my life. I lean forwards and curl my top lip. Those Xanax might be kicking in already. Or maybe it's the 400ml of vodka I downed before leaving the house.

"I've already told them." I sneer. "And something else you might like to keep in mind. I know *all* about the Dexfenfluramine you smuggled into the country. I suggest, if you want to retain your reputation as a good Samaritan, you will do as I ask."

Karter sits behind his desk again and picks up his phone. He stares at me with his finger holding down the hook. Why is he even bothering to think about this? He knows his career would blow up in one big mushroom cloud if this information got out.

Karter's nostrils flare. He lifts his finger off the hook and presses a button. "Freda, can you please book the earliest possible flight to Melbourne, Australia, for my lovely wife?"

I smile, hang my handbag over my shoulder, and adjust my left bra strap. I hold out my hand for Karter to shake. "Nice doing business with you, Dr. Schwörer."

Karter stares. His eyes glaze with defeat.

I shrug, swivel round on my heel, and stride out of the office with a victorious smile on my face. Never in my life have I had the confidence to do what I just did. Today is the beginning of a new life. A life in which *I* will be the manipulator and acquire every single thing I desire.

And I will knock down everyone who gets in my way.

chapter 32

mia
ciggies and cornflakes

First thing Friday morning I have Social Sciences. When I get out of class, I notice Mick standing at the entrance of the building with his hands in his pockets, eyes searching through the crowd of students. I hold my breath. Maybe I'll walk over to him, just to see what's up.

I'm a masochist. Can't deny it.

There's something about him. Something that excites me. And I need a hit.

Mick sees me hesitating by the classroom doorway and raises his hand a bit. But he quickly puts it back down, stares me right in the eye, and flicks his head towards the exit. A flutter in my stomach silences the teenage corridor chaos in my head.

He wants to talk to me. *Me.*

I follow him behind the toilet block. Mick leans his shoulder against the brick wall and lights a ciggie. I stop about two metres away and hug my schoolbooks to my chest. Mick sniffs, takes a long drag of his ciggie, and looks at the ground.

"What?" I squint at him.

Mick laughs. "Yer comin' over for dinner next weekend."

I look at the asphalt between my feet. The sun is hitting it just right. It shimmers like black diamonds.

"And?" I say. Is this a message, or something else?

Mick's ciggie hangs from the corner of his mouth. He shrugs.

"Do you need me for something, or are you still trying to 'break' me?" I say with a smirk.

Mick's top lip twitches. He steps closer, sliding his shoulder against the wall until his breath brushes against my face. I don't move, but I look at Mick's chest. Usually I would hold his gaze, but today I'm nervous. I like him. A lot. I think he likes me too, but I'm really not sure.

Butterflies flutter in my stomach, and I let out a tiny unintentional squeak. Man! I hope he didn't hear that. How embarrassing.

Mick smiles. I think he did hear it. Oh man, really? I'm *such* a dork. He moves his face closer and closer until his lips almost touch mine.

He whispers, "I'm a cunt."

Shit, you think?

"Uh, I don't—" I whisper back, but he doesn't let me finish my sentence.

"But I'm a cunt that can't stop thinkin' 'bout ya."

My breath catches in my throat. Now I have to look up. And the butterflies in my stomach are going berserk. He likes me?

Oh my God oh my God oh my God . . .

Mick is still squinting at me with a wonky smile on his

face. Almost sad, and somehow innocently sly. A total paradox. But it suits him. I think there's a gentle person inside him. He just doesn't want to show it.

I open my mouth to speak. I want to say something sarcastic. I don't want to appear too interested. That's the way it works, right? If I don't play hard to get, he'll lose interest in me. I definitely don't want him to lose interest in me. I should tell him I'm not worth the effort, that I'm a fat cow, and that he must be trying to mess with my head.

But just as I'm about to tell him to get stuffed, he kisses me.

Mick's eyes stay open as his warm tongue slides against mine. The taste of ciggies and cornflakes fill my mouth, but his fresh aftershave balances it out. It sounds disgusting, but it's not. My stomach is doing dances. If we weren't in school, I'd take his hand and touch it to my breast. Our gaze remains locked as he gently pulls away and takes another drag of his ciggie, making sure to blow the smoke away from my face.

My top lip twitches as I try to stop myself from smiling. Mick notices, laughs a bit, and then pulls me into him for a hug that feels more like how a bloke would pat a mate on the back. But he's hugging me. Me. Hugging. Crazy.

"Meet you here after school?" Mick says.

I nod and watch him walk across the car park.

When I turn around, Kimi is standing right behind me.

"You've got to be fucking kidding me, Mia!"

chapter 33

sonia

I. 2. buckle my shoe,
3, 4, open the door ...

Numbers. Numbers are my thing. Numbers keep my life on track. Numbers are my safety net. Working with numbers keeps me calm. They're a way to occupy my brain through periods of stress . . . and criminal cravings.

But not lately. Numbers are not doing their job. I'm scared I'm going to slip. Especially now that Ibrahim is back in town.

I sit at my desk in the staff room, staring into my tuna salad. Going over and over the possible reasons he would still be here.

What proof do I have? A faint army-boot footprint in my hallway? A stapled fertilizer bag in my shed? Mick claiming he didn't clean the kitchen? It's all pretty telling, even if not solid proof. The sole of that army boot has collided with my head more times than I can count. It's Ibrahim's foot-print for sure. He slipped up. He missed one. Or maybe it was Mick's footprint. Maybe I'm mistaken about the bag of fertilizer and I never noticed it before. It's true I have tried to stay out of the shed lately. And maybe Mick is denying cleaning the kitchen simply because he— I shake my head. I can't find a logical reason for that.

Maybe *I* cleaned the kitchen and forgot? Could I have experienced something similar to the other night in bed with Nash? If not, what was Ibrahim doing in the house? And why doesn't he want me to know he's back? Is he planning something with Mick? Is that why he has a stash of push daggers in his room? Trying to keep it a secret from me just in case I try to get him caught again? Or what if he's planning a kill? But who? All the old crew are dead or crippled, and the ones that are left in action would be hanging on Ibrahim's every word like their lives depend on it.

Well, their lives do depend on it. I scoff. Realize I may be muttering aloud to myself. I look around me, making sure there aren't any teachers in earshot. No. I think I'm okay.

What if . . . what if he wants to kill . . . me? I wouldn't put it past him. I betrayed him. And though I would never do that again, obviously he doesn't truly know how much I regret it. Maybe his desire to look the other way to "preserve me" has reached an expiry date. And if it's my life he's waiting for the perfect time to expire, and he's been in the house, why hasn't he gotten rid of the pistol I keep hidden by the front door? He's not stupid. It's not something a man like Ibrahim would overlook.

I'm still staring at my salad when Nash kisses my head. I jump in my seat.

"Sorry, mate," he says.

I spin around and smile. "Me too." If only the smile signified genuine happiness instead of adulterated worry.

Nash sits on the edge of my desk and peels a banana,

takes a bite, mumbling something with a shrug I can't comprehend.

I *tsk* in jest. "Say that again?"

Nash takes a deep breath. It whistles through his nostrils. "Mia is on drugs."

I widen my eyes in fake shock, then nod when I realize he probably already assumes I've thought the same. "Makes sense," I say.

"Makes sense?" Nash says a little too loudly, then lowers his volume. "What makes you say that?"

"She's trying to find an easy way to get thin. I knew it the instant I saw her dancing on your kitchen counter."

Nash sighs. "I confronted her about it. But she has an excuse for everything. I don't know. What do you reckon?"

"I don't think you should beat yourself up over this," I say. "There isn't much else you can do right now."

Nash nods and takes another bite of his banana. I watch as he squashes it to the roof of his mouth. I listen for the squish—it mixing with his saliva—and the swallow—the sound of fear when my victims see the knife. My heart rate slows as if I'm entering a meditative state.

I rest my hand on Nash's knee trying to stay focused on the image of a potential kill. It feels so calming . . . so right.

Nash slides off my desk and into a chair. He rubs his forehead, and then his beard. "What do you reckon I should do?"

What should he do? I snap out of my reverie. If only I had someone I could ask that very same question. I take a mouthful of salad to buy myself a moment to think. But I believe Mia being on drugs is the least of his problems right now. Something is not gelling for me regarding Celeste's claim that Mia is another man's daughter. Ibrahim and I were a part of their lives so much so that I can't remember a time when he and I did anything without them. And we were all so close. A family. I'm sure I would have noticed if Celeste had been raped. An event like that cannot be hidden from a woman's face. And even if, somehow, she did manage to hide it, why would she want to? What was she afraid of?

I go out on a limb and tell Nash my thoughts. I don't want to instill an unwarranted sense of suspicion; he's got enough to worry about, but I can't just keep these thoughts to myself. If the tables were turned, I'd expect the same from him.

"I think you're doing fine. But I also think there is something more serious you should consider." I pause and wipe my mouth with a serviette. "I'd investigate what Celeste told you a little further."

Nash squints at me and flops his banana skin in my bin. "Huh?"

I fold my hands together on my desk and look at them. "I mean, I'm not convinced Celeste is telling you the truth. About Mia."

Nash scoffs. "I wouldn't put it past her."

To be honest, I thought he'd react a little more in her defense. Perhaps he really is over her? I had always thought he would have a soft spot for her regardless. I guess she really did do a number on him.

"I'm not going to tell Mia anyway." Nash crosses his arms and gazes towards the entrance of the staff room. More teachers are rolling in.

I pucker my brow and consider telling him it's a bad idea to keep such a big secret from her, but I do understand why. Putting myself in his shoes, I'd probably feel the same way. I'd want to be my son's mother for as long as possible.

"I'm also going to insist Celeste keep it a secret for now too."

Now this, I must oppose.

"Nash, no. If it is true, she has to know."

"It'll kill her. Not to mention, she'll probably try to run away."

"Run away?"

"Yeah. Why are you saying it like that?"

"I don't think she would. She's seventeen. If she intends to leave, she can do it legitimately. And she doesn't seem the type to want to support herself yet."

Nash *tsks*, and makes a move to get out of his seat. I reach for him and grab his elbow. "Sit down. I'm sorry. I'm just—"

"You're just what? Ever since that morning Celeste called me you've been really cold. You're not jealous of her, are you?"

I laugh. "Of course not. If you took a moment to ask how *I* am, then maybe you wouldn't be making such an assumption."

Nash rubs his hands over his face and sits back down. He sighs. "You're right. What happened? You said something about guns?"

"Shh!"

"Sorry."

"No. Knives," I whisper, leaning forwards. That word slipping through my lips gives me goose bumps.

"So he has a few knives. He's a street-wise kid. He's probably trying to protect himself."

I shake my head and lean in closer. "He has *lots* of knives. Military knives."

"So . . . he's selling them?"

I wonder whether I should tell him. Maybe it's the only way. I trust Nash. A lot more than I have trusted anyone my entire life. Maybe it's time to let him in completely. I need him.

I *love* him. Maybe not as much as I loved Ibrahim, but I'd do anything to protect him.

"Nash." I clear my throat. "I have a feeling he's selling them for Ibrahim."

Nash slowly leans backwards, puts his hands behind his head, looks at the ceiling, and takes a deep breath. His seat creaks as he leans forwards again, exhales, and rests his elbows on his knees. "He's . . . *back*?"

I nod and dig my front teeth into the tip of my tongue.

Nash coughs and says, "Fuck."

chapter 39

mia

no. way.

When I turn around to see Kimi sneering at me, I laugh.
She has her hand on her hips and a frown so deep her face
looks like clay. Talk about drama queen. What's the issue
now?

"How long have you been watching me?" I say.

"Does it fucking matter?" Kimi cranes her neck forwards,
and her nostrils flare.

I step closer in defense. "Yeah, man, it matters. Just 'cause
I'm in on your shitty little revenge mission doesn't mean I
need to spend every second of my life with you. Gimme
some space."

"You're kidding, right? You really think I want to be with
you all the time, and that's why I'm pissed off I saw you
with Mick?"

I swallow and shrug. Maybe I'm reading too far into it.
We haven't been friends long. Hell, I don't even know if
this is even called a friendship. What exactly is it? And who
does she think she is speaking to me like this? Do I have
a tattoo on my forehead that says "I'm a weak geek, please
walk all over me?" I mean, come on.

"I'm pissed off because this messes with my shit."

"How is Mick kissing me messing with your shit?" I throw my arms in the air. Maybe it's a little overdramatic, but I can't help it. Kimi makes the entire world seem melodramatic. The least I can do is try to fit in when I'm around her. I chuckle to myself.

Kimi tosses her bag on the ground and pulls up her T-shirt to flash me her massive scar. "Because of *this*, Mia."

I groan. Again with the tragedy that is a scar. "Whaddaya mean?" I look at her stomach and then at Kimi's sneer. I want to physically pinch it off her face.

"What do I mean? What I mean is your little fuck buddy did this, that's what I mean."

I glare at her. "What?"

No. Way. Mick can be a dick sometimes, but I know he wouldn't do something like this. Why would he?

"Yeah. He's the one. Mick's the one I want you to fuck up."

chapter 35

mick
can't avoid that fuckin' stain no more

I wouldn't normally sit 'ere. On the creaky back porch. So close to the stain. But I need to get me shit together. I can't be feelin' all these pussy shit feelin's over a fuckin' stain, when I need to figure out a way to sell these fuckin' knives. I should just tell me mum what's goin' down. She'd be able to help me sort it out. I know that. But she's been tryin' so damn fuckin' hard to be normal. I don't wanna set 'er back. She deserves to have a normal life.

She deserves to be free.

I light a smoke. Stare at the half-filled hole in the grass where me toy truck was dug up. It reminds me of me fucked-up dad. He used to drag me along the driveway on that truck. He dragged me 'cause the wheels were clogged with dirt, 'cause I'd always be riding through the fuckin' mud 'n' pretendin' I was on an army tank bein' shot at in Afghanistan. The wheels stopped turnin'. The scrapin' sound of plastic on the concrete meant I was in for it. That scrapin' sound has echoed in me ears for fuckin' years. Once, me dad pulled too fast and hard, and I toppled over, grazing me hands 'n' knees.

He screamed 'n' yelled 'n' kicked me 'n' shit.

I cried.

It was the last time I ever cried in front of me dad. 'Cause whenever I cried, me mum would get a beat'n, accused of bringin' up a "pussy-shit," and then forced her to handle the next job "solo" as a "plea for salvation."

"Prove to me that you're devoted," he would say. "And then I'll keep my hands clear of your face. Is it a deal, Ebedi öpücük?"

That last job put me mum in lockup. Shut in a cell for three fuckin' weeks. Me alone with Dad. In this house. Thank fuckin' Christ he was hardly ever home. But Mum coulda been put away for twenny fuckin' years. But the cops offered her a deal. She took it. They tapped her phone, 'n' hid cameras in the house.

There was never a next job.

Dad found out.

Beat Mum to a pulp, put her in hospital with ten broken bones, and then he fucked off. To I-don't-give-a-fuck where.

She almost died.

Me *mum* almost died.

That was four years ago. I promised meself I wouldn't let meself love her no more. So that the next time she got hurt, I just wouldn't give a shit.

But ya know, some-fuckin'-times, no matter how thick 'n' tall you build the fuckin' wall, it doesn't help jack shit. Because when Dad had someone follow me to school a month ago, to tell me he was back, and that if I didn't do what he asked he would kill Mum, that wall didn't stop me from agreein', did it?

I didn't even ask why.

I was shittin' bricks. What else was I s'posed to do? Ask for a reason? I'd have me head fuckin' kicked in. "You don't say no to Ibrahim." I've heard me mum say it a million times.

You don't ask Dad questions. You just take his orders.

But it's gotta end.

It's time to fuck the cunt up. I've already proven I can pull the wool over the cops' eyes by doing stupid jobs here 'n' there for 'im. And if I can fool the law, there's no fuckin' reason why I can't fool Dad too. And whaddav I got to lose anyway? It's not like we're gonna be free of this lifestyle by just askin'.

Once you're in it, you're in it until you kill or be killed.

I take another drag of me smoke, drop it on the ground, 'n' scrape it into the grass with me heel.

The fly wire squeaks behind me, 'n' footsteps vibrate the porch.

Mum rests her hand on me shoulder. I lean me head against it and close me eyes.

"I'm sorry," I whisper. I am. I mean it. I'm sorry for everythin'. Even the stuff I can't control.

Mum kneels down 'n' sits next to me. Her feet dangle a bit above the ground. Mine don't. I can feel her smile. Somethin' always tingles in me chest when she does.

"I know," Mum says. "So am I. I know I wasn't much of a mother to you." Mum rests her hands in her lap 'n' squints at the shed. "But I'm really trying now."

I shrug. "I haven't been much of a son."

We both stare at the shed in silence. That fuckin' shed. Me dad's playhouse. I can't figure out how me mum can stomach goin' in there. I was never told what went down in that shed in the middle of so many fuckin' nights. But I had an idea. Especially the night of the bloodstain on the porch. I had just turned ten, 'n' Mum came in to tuck me in. She smelled of soap. She'd cleaned herself up. But she'd missed a smear of blood on her neck. And I knew, somehow, that it wasn't hers.

"You sure you're okay with Mia coming over?" Mum clicks her tongue, pushing her shoulder into me shoulder 'n' nudging me sideways.

"Yeah. Should be good." I smile and nod. I haven't seen Mia in a week. She ditched me that day I kissed 'er. Maybe I scared 'er off. But I don't understand how I coulda.

I thought she liked me.

It looked like she liked me.

I guess I'll find out when they get here.

My stomach goes all fucked up.

I think I'm nervous.

I think . . . I love 'er.

chapter 36

mia
i'm done

Dad and I stare at Sonia's front door. We're here for dinner. I've been avoiding Mick the entire week, and I'm shitting myself about seeing him again. I really like him. But after what Kimi said, I feel like I should hang low for a bit. At least until I figure out if it's true. What if they were, you know, together, and he cracked it over her splitting up with him or something? That shit is scary.

But right now I have a bigger problem. He's gonna see me. In like, one minute. Is he gonna be pissed with me? Just because he kissed me doesn't mean I need to see him all the time, right? I could act normal. Like I didn't realize it'd been so long. Is that lame?

I glance at Dad. I'm a bit sluggish and uneasy from another comedown off the pills. Dad's constantly swallowing and adjusting his collar. We're a good pair. I internally giggle.

"What are you all worked up about?" I say. I can't help myself. When it comes to Dad, all the snide remarks I bottle up each day squirt from my lips like I'm spitting up milk. I immediately apologize. But it turns out he didn't even hear me.

Dad clears his throat and straightens his back, turns his head to face me.

"Huh? What?"

I scrunch up my nose. "You look nervous."

"Nah." He shakes his head as if to convince himself. "I'm not."

"Then ring the doorbell?"

"Hmm? Oh."

Dad presses the doorbell and shakes his arms. It rings the tune of *Somewhere over the Rainbow*. I smile as I remember the story she told us in class about how she got into maths. Dad rubs his temples.

So weird.

Mick answers the door. Shit. He's dressed in a nice black shirt and smells like that fresh aftershave stuff. Mick smiles at me quickly, then shakes Dad's hand. He glances at me again, for a tenth of a second, before he clears his throat and swings the door wide open for us to enter.

What is it with men and throat-clearing?

For a moment I forget that Kimi asked me to pretend I don't know what Mick did. For a moment I forget whether it's worth the risk asking Mick if it's true. What if Kimi is totally bullshitting me? Mick must already be so pissed that I stood him up last Friday after school. But what was I supposed to do? Kimi plunked me at a crossroads.

Mick leads us to the kitchen, where Sonia is decked out in a bright-yellow apron, already serving her traditional Turkish specialties on the table. Anise and bay leaves overwhelm my senses.

Sonia rests what seems to be the last dish on the table, wipes her hands on her apron, and flings her arms in the air like a typical Turkish mama.

"Guys! Just in time."

I've never seen her so "domestic" before. Is it all an act for Dad? What's going on? Both Dad and Sonia are acting really weird. Maybe they had a fight or something.

Sonia kisses Dad and me on each cheek and gestures for Mick to pull out a chair for each of us. He obliges, makes a wonky smile, and clears his throat. Again. For real?

Nobody speaks.

We all just sit. And dig into the food. No one looks up from their plates except for me, when I ask Dad to pass the Baba Ghanoush. The swish of saliva in everybody's mouths echoes through the kitchen. The tension is hanging in the air like my own flab—thick.

"Nice food, Sonia," I say, to try to break the ice. "Thanks for having us."

Sonia lifts her head with a really fake smile and rests her knife and fork on the side of her plate.

"Thank you, Mia. Please, eat as much as you can, there's—"

Dad frowns at Sonia. She frowns back in question until it seems to dawn on her what he means. I can't believe this. He's doing it again. Why can't he just leave my weight alone? How *dare* Dad make an issue about it *here*?

Sonia's bottom lip trembles slightly, but she stops it by forcing an even tighter smile than before. Mick doesn't look up at all. He just keeps chewing, facing his plate. But then he reaches under the table and squeezes my knee.

"Thanks, but I'm full," I say, and pull my knee away from Mick's hand. My stomach sinks. I push my chair backwards and stand up. "Excuse me."

I gotta get out of this room before I cry in front of everyone.

I can hear everyone's breath stop as I walk out.

Once I get into the hallway, the tears surface. I try to hold them in, but it's not going to happen this time. This whole thing with Mick and Kimi has sucked all the grit from my soul. I wanted friends and I got morons. Serves me right. I guess I'm a moron too. I probably deserve them. I probably deserve being this fat too. Payback for all the shit I put on people at school when I was skinny and cool and good-looking, and thought I could get away with everything and anything. I tell you, being fat is a real eye-opener. You really discover who your friends are. And in my case, that's nobody. But that's my fault. Back then, I didn't want friends. I wanted people to fear me. And that's what I got, I guess. At least I can say I got what I wanted. But be careful what you wish for and all that, right?

I go to the bathroom to get some space. From Dad, from Mick, from myself. I pull my last two pills from my pocket and sit on the edge of the bathtub. I push the two pills around in my palm, whispering, "round and round the garden, like a teddy bear, one step, two steps, tickle under there." I close my fist around the pills and stand up.

Fuck this. Fuck these stupid drugs. And my stupid self-hatred.

It's bad news, man.

It's time to stick up for myself—to *look after* myself. No more bullshit. No more easy way out of anything anymore. The only way out of a sewer is to swim through the shit, right? And who gives a toss if my mum sees me like this? If she wants to inflict her fitness torment on me, I will just say no. If she makes my life a living hell for saying no, I will just leave. I'm old enough. I've got skills. I'm not an idiot. I would cope.

And all Mum has got to look forwards to nowadays is the knife. She doesn't even need it. She makes herself out to be tough, but she's not. She's weak. And she's totally fucked up her life by making stupid decisions. Fuck that. At least I'm still young. And I have plenty of time to make sure I don't become as shallow as her.

Sometimes I think my mother's actions are uglier than my own reflection.

I hold my fist over the toilet bowl and squeeze my eyes shut. I drop the pills into it, flush the toilet, take a deep breath.

I'm gonna have some of that awesome baklava Sonia made without feeling guilty. I deserve it. And I should allow myself to eat the forbidden fruit once in a while. Especially if I am a guest in someone's house.

That's *my* call. No one else's.

I open the bathroom door, and Mick is leaning his back

against the corridor wall opposite me, hands in his pockets. I freeze.

"Where've ya been all week?" Mick steps closer and tries to take my hand. I pull it away. I don't know if that's a good call. I actually want him to take my hand. Why am I letting Kimi's shit get in the way of that? Why can't I bring myself to just ask him straight?

Mick props himself against the wall with both hands, locking me between his arms, his baklava breath on my face.

I blink and look towards the front door without moving my head. "I . . . I had homework."

"Homework?" Mick smiles.

"Uh-huh."

"That's bullshit."

We stare at each other in silence. Yup, he's pissed at me. Is he going to fuck me up now too? My heart beats a little faster than usual. I'm not sure if I'm scared or if this is getting me excited.

But then he surprises me.

He steps back and lets me move.

I take the opportunity to slip out of this awkward situation. I'm pretty sure if I stayed to talk to him about it, we'd both end up saying stupid shit that didn't even make sense, to try to protect ourselves from seeming guilty.

"I'm gonna get dessert," I say. I can feel Mick's stare as I walk towards the kitchen. But just as I reach out to push the kitchen door open, Mick says my name as if he might choke on it.

I pause without turning around.

"Ya wanna see me room?" Mick says quietly and sniffs.

I turn around to face him and smile, tight-lipped. "Why?"

"Why are you so scared of me all of a sudden?"

"I'm not."

"Whaddav I done? Jus' tell me what I done."

I shrug. "Nothing."

Mick twists his mouth and puts his hands in his pockets. He hangs his head, and mumbles something I think sounds like "fucking cunt."

"What did you just call me?" Typical. And I was really beginning to think he had a heart hidden in there somewhere.

"I didn't call you anything."

"Sounded like it."

"Wasn't 'bout you."

Yeah, right. I nod and bite the inside of my cheek.

"Can ya jus' come into me room for a minute? I jus' wanna talk to ya."

I grit my teeth, nod, and step towards the door Mick points to.

Mick's room looks like a dungeon out of a theme park. I can't help but smile at the creativity.

"Cool," I say.

Mick sits on the edge of his bed and smiles too. What is all this about? Are we both pretending to be okay with each other now? And we haven't technically had an argument. Are we even a thing?

"Look." I take a deep breath and exhale through my teeth. It causes a slight whistle and puffs up my lips. I made a pledge to myself just now, to be strong. So that's what I'm going to do. I need to be adult about it. Just say what's on my mind. I can't keep going like this without clearing the air. I owe it to myself to know that truth, and I owe it to him to know where we stand with each other.

"I like you. A lot," I say. "But I found something out. About you."

Mick stands and crosses his arms.

"And I don't know what to think. I'm not supposed to say anything about it. But I can't—" I shake my head and pick at my thumbnail. "I can't *not* say anything. It's driving me nuts. And I—"

Mick's nostrils flare as he smiles. "What?"

"You know that girl at school I've been hanging with?"

"What, the Jap chick?"

I nod. I don't really like the way he spits "Jap." Makes me think that what Kimi said is true. I stare right into Mick's eyes to see if his pupils dilate. I heard somewhere that that's what happens when you lie. But they don't. Either he didn't do the shit she said, or he's a pro at this.

"Well, she said you threatened to rape her if she didn't let you *cut* her. She said you're a psychopath. That you get off on seeing blood."

Now that I've said it out loud, I realize how ridiculous it sounds.

Mick laughs. A lot. So much so that he clutches at his stomach and falls backwards onto his bed.

"You're fuckin' kidding me, right?"

I bite my bottom lip and shake my head.

"Fuck me! That chick spun some serious shit on ya. I hardly even know the bitch." Mick runs his hands over his head and swings his body into a sitting position at the edge of the bed. "You really believe I'd want to stick my dick into that skanky whore?"

"I—" My bottom lip trembles. So he denies wanting to rape her, but he hasn't said anything about the cutting. Should I read into that? And does he really have to call Kimi names? I know it's sort of just his way, and that Kimi isn't all that innocent, but it makes me feel even queasier than hearing him call *me* that stuff. If he doesn't know her, what right does he have calling her a skanky whore?

Mick breathes heavily through his nose as if to try to calm himself down. He steps closer to me and gently takes my cheeks in his hands. I look into his eyes. And all I can see in them is pain. Why does he have to be so mean all the time? I don't get it.

Maybe we're both broken.

Maybe we're two halves of the same stone.

Maybe we're in each other's lives now, to help each other become whole again, and I'm just being a self-centered bitch jumping to stupid conclusions.

Mick moves in closer. I let him. He licks my top lip, and then sucks it into his mouth, and right before I close my eyes, to let myself slip into his strange but comforting warmth, I glance towards the floor beside his bed and notice a photo of that man. That *same* man from the photo in Kimi's house, and in that footy photo of Dad's.

I gasp and pull away. I kneel on the floor and pick up the frame. I hold it tightly in both hands, and stare at it for a moment before jumping to my feet and shoving it into Mick's chest. "Who the fuck *is* this guy?"

Mick looks confused, then snatches the frame from my hands. He glances at it, and then at me.

"It's me dad. What's the fuckin' problem?"

Mick searches my eyes. I do the same to him.

"Ya know him?" Mick says, then flings the frame onto his bed. I pick it up again. I stare at it for ages, trying to convince myself I've made a mistake. I chew my bottom lip until I realize it hurts.

"Mia. What the fuck?"

I look up and say, "He used to be my dad's best mate. He's in all his footy photos at home. Did you know this?"

"Uh . . . nah, I didn't, but so? What's with the freak-out?"

"I saw a photo of him in Kimi's bedroom too."

Mick rubs his hands over his head. "What?" His voice goes really low.

"I know. Weird, right?"

Mick stares out his window.

"I think—"

"What?"

I shake my head. "I'm not sure, but I think he might be her foster dad."

Mick grabs his head, kicks his wall, and shouts, "Fuckin' arsehole cunt!"

I stare at his knuckles turning white.

"What's going on?" I say as quietly as possible.

"Ya can't get involved. Okay? Stay out of it. Forget what ya saw."

"What do you mean?" I can't just forget what I saw. His face is all over my house. Something is going on. And it's weird.

"It's . . . fuck, Mia, ya 'ave no idea what this means."

"Explain it then."

"I can't."

"Why?"

"Because . . ."

"Mick, I'm not your little sister. Whatever it is, I can handle it, alright?"

Mick's jaw is clenched; he's staring straight into my eyes. I can see he wants to tell me something. What's stopping him? Is it really so bad?

"I know—" I hesitate and reach for Mick's hand, but decide against it and cross my arms instead. "I know we're kinda new, but you can trust me, you know. You're the only person that's ever—" I shrug, sigh, hang my head.

"I know," Mick says with a slight laugh. "I feel the same about you too."

I nod, smile, step closer, and lean into Mick's chest. His heart beats against my right cheek. It's fast but certain, a steady beat. I should trust him. Not push. I have never seen him talk to anyone in school. Ever. But he talked to me. And now I'm in his bedroom. That's something. And the closer we get, the more he'll tell me. I have to be patient. If I care about him, and he cares about me, I have to wait this out.

But something weird is definitely going on here. Everyone in this house seems to be stepping on eggshells.

"Mia," Mick whispers. "Why the fuck didjya get involved with this chick?" He wraps his arms around me and kisses me on the top of my head. He holds me tightly. I don't want to move. I close my eyes and try to slow my breathing down so it matches the way Mick's heartbeat slows.

"Me dad. He's—" Mick pauses and leans his head against mine. Something is breaking his heart. I can sense it. So much so that I imagine hearing it crack in his chest.

"He's a criminal. A fuckin' drug lord."

My eyes flick open, but I don't move.

Mick swallows. "He's hiding behind an alias since the cops almost caught him in the middle of a fucked-up deal. I guess now I know where he is." Mick laughs. "He used to always say that no one ever thinks to look in their own backyard. Guess I'm as big a fuckwit as everyone else."

I pull away slowly. Is he for real? And my dad played footy with this guy?

"Okay," I stammer. "What's this all got to do with you? And why is Kimi out to get you? Do you think she's, uh—"

Mick nods. "I'm workin' with 'im."

"What!"

"Shh! Keep your fuckin' voice down."

I cup a hand over my mouth and look at the picture of

Mick's dad on the bed. He looks so kind and friendly. A real family man with a big white smile.

Mick's eyes are rimmed with tears. He sits on the bed and lets himself fall backwards. He stares at the ceiling with his hands on his head.

"I have to. I've got no choice. If I don't do what he asks, he'll—"

"He'll what?" Great. His dad is blackmailing his own son?

"Doesn't matter. But I've got this stash of fucking bullshit weapons that I have to exchange for coke by the end of the month. And if I don't do it, then I'm fucked. And it won't just be me who suffers."

"And it's your *dad*? Your dad who's asking you to do this?"

Mick nods. "He's a heartless fuckin' cunt who almost—"

"We should tell my dad. I mean, maybe he can help you. I mean, they used to be really close, I think."

Now I understand why Dad never speaks about him.

Mick jolts upright shaking his head. "No way. No fuckin' way."

"Why not? This shit, it's . . . you wanna go to prison?"

Mick takes a deep breath, grabs the waistline of my jeans, and pulls me onto the bed next to him. "If I tell ya everythin', ya have to promise ya won't breathe a fuckin' word of it."

Maybe if Mick can trust me, I'll be able to convince him to do the right thing. So I agree. "I won't," I say. "I won't say anything. But my dad, he can help. I'm sure he can. If you ever want him to."

Mick stands up and walks to the window. He closes the curtains over the already closed blinds as if it's somehow going to make the room soundproof.

"No, he can't. He can't because me mum can't know about this."

"But your mum is married to your dad. Surely she knows what he is."

"Yeah. She does. And she keeps a pistol hidden by the fuckin' front door. Every day, she checks it's still there. And loaded."

I gulp. "What are you saying?"

"What I'm sayin' is, me dad has threatened to, ya know, do some fucked-up shit if I don't do what he asks."

"What, you mean—" I pause, then mouth, "murder?"

Mick stands still, doesn't even blink, but he doesn't have to say a thing. My hands tremble, and I have a huge craving for a pill. Why did I flush them down the toilet? Today of all fucking days? I suddenly feel faint and break into a light sweat. I have to lower myself to the floor. It feels safer here somehow.

Mick kneels next to me. Silent but caring. He moves the hair away from my eyes and squeezes the back of my neck. He grabs an almost empty bottle of water from the floor, spins the cap off, and hands it to me. I take it and drink the two mouthfuls that are left.

"You have to do something," I say. "You have to get outta this."

"It's okay. He promised to lay off as soon as I get this one thing done for him."

"One thing? Is it possible for it to just be one thing and then over? I've seen those true-crime TV series about this stuff. Would he really let you off the hook?"

Mick shrugs.

"You really think he'd do something so drastic as killing your mum if you didn't? It sounds crazy. There's no way he'd kill your mum. He's just trying to get the most out of you, right?"

"I dunno. But I can't let me mum find out about this. It'd destroy 'er if she knew he was fuckin' with me like he did with her. She'd do something that she'd regret. I know 'er."

I lean my back against the edge of the bed.

I'm in this now.

I'm mixed up with a criminal. Oh my God.

Now what do I do? I can't just run away from it and pretend it's not happening. I mean, how do I even act around Dad now? I can't just blurt out, "Hey, dad, did you know that your ex-footy mate wants to kill your girlfriend?"

This is insane.

"I want to help," I say, before I've even thought about the consequences. "Let me help you."

Mick stares at the wall for a moment and nods, "Maybe ya can." His eyes shine, and it worries me. I hope he doesn't ask me to do anything with those weapons he was talking about. "Maybe ya could try 'n' find out if Kimi has anythin' to do with me dad's shit."

Whoa. Okay. I'm sorta relieved he didn't ask me to

commit a crime, but this is still a little out of my league. I've never tried to manipulate anyone in my life.

"How?" I say. I sound like an idiot. A wimp. I take a deep breath and repeat the question with a bit more confidence.

"Jus' do what yer already doin'." Mick smirks. "Play 'er. Like she's playin' *you*."

chapter 37

mick

sometimes *fuck* means shit all

I help me mum clean up the kitchen after dinner.

I'm dryin' dishes.

She's washin' 'em.

We get to the cutlery.

She always leaves 'em last.

Her hand movements get slower.

She slides the soapy sponge up 'n' down the blades of the knives.

A smile creeps up on 'er face.

Like she don't even know it's there.

"Mum," I say.

She don't say nothin'.

"Mum," I say a bit louder.

I give her shoe a gentle kick.

She stops what she's doin'.

Looks at me in shock.

And 'er smile becomes tears.

I put the tea towel down.

And walk out the back door.

chapter 38

sonia

knives + throats + blood = bliss

I'm alone in the house. The kitchen is clean. I turned the knives upside down in the dish rack so only the handles are visible. I stare at them. Fighting the urge to turn them around. I take a deep breath, and it quivers on the way out. I cover my mouth with my hand. I hold that hand in place with my other hand.

I scream.

I scream again.

I can't handle it anymore.

I pull a carving knife out of the dish rack, the extended ting of the steel as it brushes against the other cutlery initiates calm.

I look at my reflection in the blade. Stare at my eyes staring back at me in disgust. When I thought Ibrahim had left for good, I thought I could get through this. But now that he's back, I can't stop thinking about him.

Every night, for the past week, I've been standing in the shed for hours, smoking cigarettes, hoping he'd drop by.

Before I can stop myself with my usual rationale, I run the blade of the knife across the top of my left arm. The warm soothing blood oozes from my skin and releases the pressure in my head as if I've injected myself with a sedative.

I drop the knife to the floor. It clangs on the tiles. I spread blood all over my arm and admire the patterns it makes on my skin.

Ibrahim. I miss you.

chapter 39

mia
and it all starts to make sense

I skip class on Monday and lie flat on my back in the middle of the old football field, the tips of the overgrown grass gold and crispy from the sun. I flick off my shoes with my toes and shade my eyes with my right arm. I lie still, in silence, until the air around me begins to whistle lullabies, and anonymous insects take on the roles of backup singers.

I didn't cave. Didn't take another pill. I feel like I've run a marathon. And my hands are bit shaky. But I also feel good about myself for once, despite feeling so run-down. I was only taking the pills on and off for two weeks, so it can't get any worse, can it?

I think about the weekend. About the dizziness I felt when I mouthed "murder." What does this say about me? It's a scary thought. It's not TV. It's real. And a part of *my* life.

I am needed. Despite what I look like. And that feels good.

Is it weird that it excites me? Could it be that the possibility of danger just hasn't hit me yet? Or could it be that I am, deep down, one of *them*? The kind of person that gets a thrill from the chase?

I've seen on TV how organized crime can get totally out of control. I've seen how a happy family household can turn into a bloody slaughterhouse within seconds. I've seen how one stupid mistake, one stupid little fuckup, can turn into the murder of those in its wake.

Anything could happen now. Couldn't it?

Once I start this.

And—

Man, *what* am I *thinking*?

I take a deep breath. Some birds tweet in the background. Someone approaches.

"I knew you'd be here."

I remove my arm from my face and open my eyes. Kimi is hovering over me. I sit up.

"How?"

Kimi shrugs. "Just did." She kneels down next to me and tilts her head. She strokes my cheek. "You look pretty in the sunlight."

I want to slap her hand away, but then I realize this could be the perfect opportunity to make Kimi trust me and tell me what I need to know.

I smile and lean my head into her hand. For a split second, she looks surprised. Her breath shudders and she inches forwards. I close my eyes. I know what she wants. I've known ever since the day she pushed me against her dresser. I don't know what I'm scared of. The fact that I've never been with a girl before, or that I'm starting to like the idea of it?

I'm just going to do it. It's the only way to figure out where Kimi stands anyway.

Kimi leans over me, inches closer to my lips. I close my eyes. She smells like a mix of jasmine and fairy floss. The heat of her breath brushes against my lips right before she kisses me. Lips closed. Gentle, like we're two little sisters.

Kimi hovers her face above mine without touching. Her breath stops for a moment, then she kisses me again. This time she parts my lips with her tongue. She tastes like peach schnapps.

My crotch starts to burn and pulsate. I want more. But I'm scared. Not of her touching me. But of me liking it so much that I lose sight of what I'm trying to do.

I need to make this about her. Not me. So I slip my hand between Kimi's legs and under her knickers. Kimi groans, rolls onto her back, and spreads her legs wider. Now I'm on top of her and have one of her legs between mine. She's so wet that my forefingers slip inside her with hardly any force.

She fingers at the waistband of my tracksuit.

"Pull them down," she whispers.

"Out here?"

"Why not?"

"Why don't you just—" I bend over and thrust my tongue into Kimi's mouth, then gently bite her bottom lip "—let me make *you* come."

Now I am in control. It feels like a miracle. Is it really this easy? Is this maybe all Kimi has wanted all along? To get into my pants?

Breathless, Kimi pulls the collar of her T-shirt into her mouth and bites it. I flick my fingers over her clit until she comes. She arches her back and takes my hand from between her legs and licks my fingers.

Oh. My. God. That is so disgusting. The thought of tasting myself makes me want to gag, but I hide it behind a forced "sexy" smile.

Kimi rolls over onto her stomach and starts to laugh.

I chuckle a bit. I can't believe I just had lesbian sex. And pretty much enjoyed it (except for that last bit, of course.) I don't know why she's laughing, but my chuckle is definitely a nervous reaction.

We lie in silence for a few minutes until I find the courage to bring up Mick.

"So, uh, are you going to tell me what I have to do now?"

"Huh?" Kimi looks to her left. "About what?"

"Mick."

"Oh, yeah." Kimi smiles, takes a deep breath, and pushes her skirt between her knees as she slowly exhales.

"Well, I don't actually want to *hurt* him. I was just winding you up. I thought you looked like the type of person who liked to, you know, punch."

"Oh, man. You're kidding me, right?" So this *was* all because she wanted to get into my pants?

"Nope. I just need something he has."

"Oh. What does he have?"

Kimi smirks, sits up, and moves her eyebrows up and down. "Some kick-arse weapons."

Whoa. Maybe she *is* doing this for Mick's dad.

I pick at a fingernail, trying to look casual, like this information isn't really that important to me.

"What do you need them for?" I say.

Kimi cranes her neck. "Do you have any idea how much money that shit is worth?"

I shrug. I'm not meant to know. "Maybe."

"If I can get them and sell them," she says, then bites her bottom lip, "then I'm set, and I can get the hell outta here."

I nod, look at my left palm, and trace my lifeline with my ring finger. Should I just ask about her connection to Ibrahim? Would she freak out? Would she call the whole thing off if she thought I was onto her?

But on the flip side, maybe I should take this chance. What if I don't find myself in this kind of situation again? I can't imagine Kimi ditching me now, but I don't think I can take that chance. Kimi seems the most relaxed I have ever seen her, and let's face it, I am in control, finally, whether she realizes this or not.

"Can I ask you a personal question?" I keep my tone as casual as possible.

Kimi lifts her arms, lies back down, and rests her head on her hands. She closes her eyes and smiles into the sun. "Sure. Shoot."

"Are you okay?" I know this is probably treading on dangerous territory, but it's the only way I'm going to get what I need. "I mean . . . at home?"

Kimi's flicks her eyes and shades them with her hand. "Why you asking me that?"

I shrug again and adopt a look of concern.

"It's just . . . those scars. I mean, if you don't want to actually hurt Mick, then I'm assuming that he didn't, you know, do that." I nod towards Kimi's stomach.

Kimi closes her eyes again and smiles tight-lipped.

Here goes.

"Has it got anything to do with your foster dad?"

Kimi's throat moves like she's swallowing a marble, and a tear falls down her left temple.

Silence.

Maybe this isn't what I thought at all. Maybe Kimi's attitude is all show.

"Is he hurting you? Is that why you need cash? To get away?"

Kimi sits up slowly, staring at nothingness. She clutches at her necklace as if she's about to yank it off, but she doesn't. She just rests her hand there. On her chest. Fingers hooked around the gold chain. It has a tiny dragon hanging from it. I wouldn't have even been able to tell what it was if I wasn't so close to her.

"If I tell you the truth"—Kimi lowers her voice—"you have to promise me, I mean really promise me, you won't tell anyone."

"Of course."

"He's not really my foster dad." She swallows. "He took me in one night. I was out of it. High. Lying on the side of the road. I'd been attacked by someone. I don't know who it was. They did this." Kimi rubs her fingers over her scar.

"Then they beat me, and, yeah, anyway, I was sure I was going to die that night. But he saved me. I've been living with him ever since." Kimi clenches her jaw.

"What's this guy's name?" Of course, I know it. But I have to seem legit.

"Dunno," she says. Kimi laughs. Which is kinda weird.

"How's that possible?"

"He won't say. I just call him Daddy."

"Daddy?" I raise my eyebrows.

"Yeah. Pretty fucked, isn't it?"

"Why didn't you just leave straight away and find a shelter or something?"

"You kidding? The guy is loaded. All I have to do is . . . do stuff for him every couple of days, and I live like a queen."

Stuff? If that stuff is what I think it is, that is fucking gross. I'm so glad Mick wants to get out of that kind of life.

We both pick at the grass.

"So how come you even bother coming to school?" I say after a few moments of silence.

"It's his cover." Kimi smiles, but immediately looks as if she regretted saying it. Sex has definitely made her vulnerable, and now I feel guilty. "Shit. Mia, you can't talk to anyone about this. I'm not supposed to say anything. I'd be totally screwed if he found out I'd even suggested he exists."

"Okay. Don't worry." I touch Kimi's knee. "What's he hiding from?"

"Fucked if I know. All I know is that I'm still alive, and I'd like to keep it that way."

"You don't have to live like this, Kimi. I can get you some help."

Kimi laughs again. "I don't need your help. I can look after myself."

So how does she know about the weapons? Does she know that he's Mick's dad?

"Uh, just out of curiosity, how did you find out Mick has these weapons?"

Kimi stares at me in silence. I can't tell whether it's fear or a pending threat shining through her eyes.

"Just overheard some phone conversation, that's all."

Something isn't quite right here. But I feel like I should back off now. Something in her voice has changed.

It's defensive.

Kimi twists her hair to the front of her shoulder and combs her fingers through it, squinting at the ground. It looks like she's biting the inside of her cheek. She's hiding something else. I know it.

"Look, are you going to help me get them or not?"

"I'm on your side, man. You don't need to get upset with me. But can I ask *you* a favour too?"

Kimi takes a deep breath and sighs like it's an apology. "Anything."

"Can you hold off on stealing that shit a bit longer?"

Kimi frowns. "Why?"

"I have a better idea to get you outta there."

chapter 90

celeste
home sweet home

I collect my Louis Vuitton luggage off the conveyor belt, contemplating going back to duty free to pick up some perfume. I have to smell perfect when I drop in to see Nash. I need him to melt. Like he used to. In the crook of my neck. *Purr*ing. We used to be the perfect couple. The couple everyone believed would go the distance, you know?

What a stupid mistake it was to leave him. If only I'd known that all Karter ever wanted me for was decoration, then I wouldn't have even bothered. Yes, I admit it, I married him for the money. I was tired of being the suburban housewife, tired of picturing myself forty years from now, old, grey, wrinkly—fat. But I married Karter over a delusion that he might help me become the next Jane Fonda. Invest some money in me starting my own fitness studio and produce some workout videos. I honestly wanted to help people become the beauty queens they'd dreamed about being since their debutant balls.

How stupid I was to think he'd want to do that for me. All he did was shape me into an accessory. One he could perpetually have hanging from his arm during public appearances.

I was gullible.

Of course he couldn't find a wife.

Anyone smart enough would have seen through his charm and run a mile. But did I? Of course not. I had my eye on the riches and got distracted. And all for what? I lost my family because I—what? Felt a little old? Midlife crisis drama? So, the boys go for the red-hot Ferrari and the girls for the red-hot post-cosmetic surgery skin abrasions.

Clever.

I deserve to be blond.

I'm never going to convince Nash to love me again. I know this. I devastated him. And he'll never forgive me for devastating Mia. How could I have been so selfish? But I honestly thought that it would only be a matter of time before she'd come running to me, begging to live with me in LA. I am shocked that she didn't. That she enjoys living with a man who has to go to high school until he retires.

How horribly sad and boring.

What happened to his aspirations?

If there is a will, there is a way. He can't blame my getting pregnant for his own decision to quit football.

So I have decided, seeing as there is no turning back, that the only way to get my family on track is to embrace who I have become—a selfish, shallow, money-sucking, life-sucking desperate housewife.

I don't regret telling Nash about the "assault." Not. One. Single. Bit. I've got nothing to lose. If it works? Bonus. If it doesn't, I've got plenty of Xanax to top myself with while anonymously accommodated in the penthouse at the Hilton.

My luggage finally comes swinging around the bend. I snatch it off the conveyor belt, wheel it out of customs, focusing straight ahead with a plastic smile on my face. Literally. I got one last Botox injection before I left. I couldn't resist.

I pause a few meters away from the sliding doors leading to the taxi line, gulp at the sensation of my tingling limbs and my spinning head.

I release my grip on my suitcase. It drops to the floor with a thud that hangs thick in my ears, and I rummage through my handbag for the Xanax. I haven't had one for forty-eight hours. I know exactly what's going on.

Withdrawal.

With trembling hands I open the bottle of pills, then shake some into my palm. A couple slip between my fingers and fall to the floor. Suffocating on my own breath, I bend down to pick them up, but the bottle slips from my hand. Pills scatter all over the hard white floor like sundried pieces of my brain.

"Shit!" I shriek, then fall to my hands and knees, scampering to gather them into a pile. I lick my middle finger and press down on a couple so they stick, then lick them off my fingers.

I taste the oily grime from the airport floor and wince.

I've consumed worse.

I sense people stare as they walk by. The sliding doors

sigh with impatience every time they open and close. I take a deep breath, close my eyes, and sit up. My black stilettoed feet slip to the side of my thighs like a kindergarten kid in a classroom.

You're not in the outback. Just buy more, I say to myself.

I quickly grab two or three more pills off the floor, secure them in my palm with three fingers, and stand up. I drop them into my purse, snap it shut, flick my hair behind my shoulders, and walk out of the airport as if nothing at all has happened.

Breathe. They will *love you again. Even if it's just pretend.*

After a detour to a chemist's with my rented dark-blue Mercedes, and half an hour squabbling with the pharmacist before bribing him with an amount of cash the man wouldn't dream of earning in one year, I head towards my old home with a full bottle of tranquilizers. I have no idea what I'm going to do when I arrive, but I've decided I'll take this one step at a time. If the courage to make an appearance escapes me, I might spend the night staring at my old front lawn. But that's okay. That's one step closer to my goal. What matters now is that I'm here, and I'm on the road to getting my life back on track, to normal, to the way it was before I appreciated how wonderful my life was. Well, in hindsight, at least I wasn't lonely.

What more does a woman need in this day and age? It's all about keeping up appearances, and everything on the surface of our life was shiny and clean.

When I reach the corner of my old street, I stop the car.

"Just take a quick look," I say to myself in the rearview mirror. "Then go to the hotel."

I roll into my street and head towards my house at 5km an hour. I notice a girl walking with a backpack in the same direction. She's unhealthily overweight and dressed in a black tracksuit, decent, but a little tattered around the ankles. The kind that reminds me of the pot-smoking days with Nash and Ibrahim. I smile at the thought, but then with a touch of pity towards the girl.

Poor thing. She could really do with a personal trainer. Maybe I can offer my services when I move back into the neighbourhood.

But wait. The girl opens the gate to my old house. And walks to the front door!

I frown. She doesn't look like the type of girl Mia would hang out with. At all. But there's something familiar about the way she moves and rummages in her schoolbag. I retrieve my mini binoculars from my handbag and lift them to my eyes.

Gasp!

She's pulling out her key, still attached to that ridiculous dog chain.

Mia? Oh my *God*. Nash, what have you done to her?

There's no way I can sit back and allow my daughter to ruin herself a second longer. Just look how ugly she has become! I must get back into their lives. Right now.

I unhook my iPhone from the hub in the dashboard, and with the edge of my right index finger text Nash.

I'm in Melbourne. Meet me at Roxy's in two hours. Or I tell her.

chapter 91

mia
i never would have guessed

I'm lying flat on my back staring at Mick's collection of boobs and arses on his bedroom ceiling.

"I think Kimi's just scared," I say. "We could use this to your advantage, babe."

Babe? Where did that come from?

Mick pulls all the knives out of his box and lines them up at the base of his bed. He hasn't seemed to notice what I called him. It's practically saying that we're officially together.

Are we? We haven't talked about it. Is it possible to be an item without declaring it to each other? Or is that too "high school?" I can't deny feeling like it has to be announced. Could I really assume that we just are?

The thought gives me tingles all over, and I imagine sliding under his bedcovers.

With him following me.

Kissing.

Mick doing to me what I did to Kimi.

I have the same burning feeling in my crotch as I did with Kimi. I slide my feet up to my bum and let my knees fall to the side. I notice that the skin over my knees isn't pulling as badly as usual. Could I have lost a bit of weight?

Mick shrugs and says, "I dunno." He hooks his thumbs into the pockets of his jeans and looks left to right at all the knives on the bed.

"What do you mean, you dunno?" What I really want is to ask Mick if he's my boyfriend, but I force myself to stay on topic. "It makes sense. We tell her who she's really living with, how much danger she could be in, and get her on our side to help you find some coke, and, you know, give her a cut from it to sell instead of your knives. We already know she can get speed."

Mick pauses and looks up. "How?"

Shit.

"Uh," I hesitate for a moment, but then realize there's no harm in telling him the truth. "She was giving me some so I could lose weight."

"What?" Mick laughs and nods. "Now, I geddit."

I sit up and shrug. "Yeah. But it's not like that. I'm not addicted to that shit or anything. And I stopped. I feel totally fine." Just as I say that my eye twitches. "Can we talk about that later?"

Mick shrugs and frowns. Could that actually be a sign of concern for my well-being?

"Okay," he says. "But can we fuck'n' trust 'er?"

"Don't you think it's worth the risk? It's either that or her trying to get your knives. And I'm not sure I can keep pretending I don't have anything to do with you because—"

Mick smiles at me. "'Cause?"

We stare at each other with smirks on our faces. Mick walks to the side of the bed, sits next to me, and wraps his right hand around the back of my neck.

We kiss. With a lot of tongue.

I can hardly catch my breath by the time we stop.

Mick stands up and continues the conversation as though it wasn't interrupted. My heart is beating as if I were still on speed.

"Maybe we can ask 'er, but I still think she needs to prove herself."

Maybe we are an item. Would he behave so comfortably if we weren't?

"How?" I say.

"Get his contacts for us?"

"You want her to snoop through his shit?"

"Yeah."

"What if she gets caught?"

Mick leans his back against his set of drawers. "If she needs the fuckin' dough to save 'er own life, then she'll do it. If she wants to get outta here so bad, she'd take whatever op she could get."

"Why would her life be in danger? She's living like a queen—she said so herself. We'd have to offer her something better than that, babe."

This time I didn't say *babe* by accident.

"Dad is a fuckin' cunt. He doesn't give a fuck about Kimi. Trust me. If she's in the way of his business, he'll just kill 'er. Slaughter 'er like a fuckin' lame horse."

I glare at him. I don't know how to respond to that. Really?

"I'm fuckin' serious," he says.

"I don't think she'll go for it." I massage my temples.

Mick half sighs and *tsks*. "Fuck. I'll just say it."

"Say what?"

"She's toying with ya."

"What do you mean?"

"What if she's actually workin' with me dad? What if he's havin' her steal the weapons *for* 'im?"

"Why would he do that? I don't understand how—"

"Mia. Fuckin' think." Mick whacks the side of his head as if it's somehow going to jump-start mine to function like a gangster's. "He hates my mother's fuckin' guts. He wants revenge because she's the one who worked with the cops to try 'n' nab 'im in the fuckin' first place. Maybe he's trying to fuck up this whole deal I have goin' with him. It makes sense. Then he gets *everything* he wants. He doesn't give a fuck that I'm his son, or that me mum is his wife. All he gives a fuck about is money. And blood." He points his finger at me and makes a popping sound like it's a gun.

"Oh."

"Yep."

I squint out the window trying to think of a solution. As if I'm even qualified to come up with one. All I can think of is to go to the cops. But if Ibrahim really is as crazy as Mick makes out, I can't see how the cops are going to be able to do anything anyway. Clearly he's escaped them plenty of times before.

"We gotta hide these somewhere else." Mick juts his chin towards the knives on his bed.

"Where?"

"I have a mate that could help."

"A mate."

"Yeah, a mate."

I don't wanna feel like this, but I think this is freaking me out a bit. I move my hair out of my eyes, and my hands start to shake. I grit my teeth, stand up, and cross my arms, so Mick doesn't see.

"I don't get how telling someone else about this is gonna help us, babe. You won't even tell your mother. I mean, she's the one in danger here, right? She deserves to know." Okay, maybe I yelled a little too loud. But I had to. The air was building up inside my chest.

Mick cranes his neck, his jaw hanging slightly open. "Will ya keep your fuckin' voice—"

Mick's bedroom door swings open and ricochets off the dresser.

"What are you two yelling about in here?" Sonia leans against the door frame and puts her hands in her pockets.

We stare at her.

Speechless.

I can't be the one to say anything. It's not my right.

"I thought ya said ya locked the fuckin' door," Mick says through gritted teeth.

"I thought I did." Honestly. I really thought I did.

"She obviously didn't," Sonia says.

"Shut the fuck up, Mum, it's got nothin' to do with ya."

"Hey!" I don't know what makes me stick up for Sonia, but Mick is way too mean to her. I really don't get it. I mean, sure, I get it, but I think he goes overboard sometimes. Sonia interrupts, flicks her hand as if it's nothing, and remains calm.

"Don't worry about it, Mia. I'm used to it. He gets it from his father." Though she's speaking to me, Sonia says this while staring directly at Mick.

Mick clenches his fists and punches the air with a roar.

"But he loves you." I whisper. I can't help it. He does. She should at least know that.

Mick shakes his head as if to tell me to stop talking.

"What's up? Spit it out," Sonia says.

"He doesn't want me to tell you." I'm getting in deeper here. And I'm probably screwing up our relationship as well. I mean, we just got started and I'm already trying to play the martyr. Am I insane? I hope he doesn't hate me after this. I hope we can still be a thing. Because I really like him. I mean, *really* like us being a thing.

"Don't. Please," Mick says, shaking his head and holding a sideways fist over his mouth.

"He doesn't want you to tell me what?" Sonia says dryly. Silence.

Sonia's trousers ruffle as she switches the weight from one foot to the other.

Mick grabs my hand. We sit on the edge of his bed. He squeezes the back of my neck and winks at me. He's letting me know it's okay. He's not getting angry. The relief flushing through me is like shedding thirty kilos and slipping into a bikini for the first time in forever.

"Why should I be worried?" Sonia says and steps inside the room properly.

She stares at the knives. Her expression doesn't even change. It's like she's looking at a set of silver spoons.

Is she for real? This is my teacher. My dad's girlfriend. And she doesn't even bat an eyelid over illegal weapons splayed all over her son's bed?

I frown at Mick in question. Mick stares at his feet. His right leg jerks up and down. Fast.

"You're working for him, aren't you?" Sonia grips the iron foot of the bed. Her knuckles go white. But her face doesn't reflect the same feelings as her hands. It's . . . freaky.

She picks up a push dagger and runs her forefinger over it, as if tracing the letter *T*. She smiles. Looks up. Lets the push dagger slip from her fingers. It clunks against one of the other knives. "Tell me."

I notice tears in Mick's eyes. He stops moving his leg and stares at her. He clutches my hand and pulls it into his lap. His squeeze is gentle but firm. Like he's telling me that everything is going to be okay.

"He wants revenge, doesn't he?" Sonia whispers.

Silence.

This is intense.

All I can do is sit and listen.

Mick's touch is the only thing holding my emotions in

check. I can't help but wonder what it would be like if this was happening to me and Dad.

"I want you to stop, Mick," Sonia says. "Whatever it is you're doing. It's got to stop. Whatever happens, happens. I just want you to be safe. You hear? I don't want you doing this anymore."

"Whaddaya mean, *anymore*?" Mick releases my hand, stands up, sticks his chest out in defense.

"I'm not stupid," Sonia says, hardly reacting to Mick's behaviour.

Mick sticks his tongue into the side of his cheek. It looks like he's biting down on it.

Sonia shifts her gaze towards me and smiles, tight-lipped. "Mia, I'm really sorry about this, but I think you should go home."

I nod and stand.

"No. Stay," Mick whispers, and touches me lightly on the elbow.

"You can't get Mia wrapped up in this mess, Mick. Use your brain. Don't be an idiot."

"Mum, ya don't get what's goin' on."

"I know a lot more than you think I do."

Sonia glares at Mick like she has the power to stare him into submission.

This is off-the-charts insane. I want to say something. I can't pretend to not be involved—it just wouldn't be right, and I can't keep secrets very long anyway. They just come out.

"Mrs. Shâd," I say. "I can't stay out of it now. It's impossible."

Sonia takes a deep breath and glares at Mick, as if this whole fiasco is his fault. "Why can't she stay out of it?"

Mick stares at me for a moment. Then nods. "Why can't you stay out of it, babe?" It's my cue.

There's no turning back now. Mick and Sonia make eye contact. For a short moment, it feels like Mick is finally letting go of the stress. There's relief in his eyes. A sad yet much needed relief.

"Well," I say, "there's this girl at school. Her name is Kimiko."

chapter 92

nash
plastic invader

The last thing I need right now is Celeste. Storming into my life again. What is she doing here so bloody early? Is she planning on telling Mia? If she does, things are going to get complicated. Mia turned to drugs. To escape the shit. It's stupid teenage shit, but I remember exactly how big all the shit seemed at that age. The past few days, though, despite her shaking hands and odd twitch of the eye, she doesn't seem as uptight. I reckon that's a sign she's come to her senses. And that would've taken courage. Courage I'm certain she had to dig to the very core of her soul to find. If Celeste goes behind my back, there's no telling how Mia will react, how she will deal with the stress next time. Maybe she'd turn to more serious drugs. I can't let that happen.

I park my car. Find the perfect spot right out in front of Roxy's. As I step onto the footpath I see Celeste in the window, tapping away at her iPhone with her bright-pink nails, intermittently sipping a latté. I bet it's a skinny decaf.

I stare.

The soles of my feet burn into the concrete. I can't move. How did she turn into this . . . this . . . object? She used to be so down-to-earth, opposed to materialistic reward, environmentally conscious, still sexy in a baggy pair of tracky daks, a T-shirt, and no makeup.

Now look at her.

A prissy plastic princess.

Celeste pauses as if she heard something, looks up from her phone, and smiles at me through the window.

Fake.

And way too white.

For some reason I'm surprised she notices me standing here at all. She stares like she can see through me.

The table she is at is small, and she bangs her hip against the edge of it as she stands up. She winces but seems to quickly overcome the pain and perform some awkward version of jazz hands—a gesture for me to hurry up and get inside so she can give me a hug. I don't smile back, but she maintains her happy-go-lucky role regardless as I head to the entrance.

Celeste oohs and ahhs, squeezing my biceps, pouting with what seems like pride over the fact that I'm still in great shape.

She hugs me. My arms hang limp at my sides. Someone would have to threaten to kill me to reciprocate Celeste's manipulative embrace.

"Oh, how much I've missed you!" Celeste pushes me away in jest, far enough to get a good look at my face, *tsk*ing in a way that I s'pose to mean "boy, does time fly."

"What do you want?" I scrape the chair on the floor as I

pull it out, sit down with a clank, and slap my wallet and keys on the table. "Get on with it. I have a busy day."

Celeste's smile fades just enough for me to notice she's trying not to react. She raises her hand to grab a waiter's attention without sitting down. A waiter waltzes over, cups his hands together in front of his clean black apron, and raises his brow at me.

"I'm not staying, mate," I say.

The waiter nods, smiles at Celeste's nervous laugh, and walks away. Roxy's is one of those rich bitch places where not ordering anything is frowned upon. He'll be back in a minute asking me to order a drink or "kindly leave."

Celeste sits down slowly, as if the chair might break. "Nash, darling. I'm so sorry for just turning up like this." She lays her hands flat on the table and slides them towards my clenched fists. I withdraw. So does Celeste with a dramatic sigh.

She looks out the window, breathing as if she's trying to stop tears. "I miss you. I miss Mia."

"Yeah, well, should've thought of that before you ran off."

"I've left him."

I scoff. "Brilliant. Good on you. Find someone richer?"

Celeste closes her eyes, and a single tear falls down her cheek at just the right moment, like she planted it there.

"Save the act, Celeste. Look at you. You're *not you*. You're not the *you* I knew, anyway."

"I can be. I can be anything you want." Celeste opens her eyes and locks on my gaze.

"What?"

"I want another chance. I'll do anything. I want my family back. Please. I'm— I'm lonely." Celeste's tears turn into theatrical gasping sobs, loud enough to turn heads and raise the eyebrows of every customer within earshot.

I slide my wallet and keys closer to my body. I want to get out of here, but instead I watch her cry. There's something about her right now. I can't take my eyes off her. Like underneath all the forged beauty lies a soul unaffected, as if her plastic mask has somehow shielded it from bad weather.

She's still there. Under there. Somewhere. But no longer reachable.

I could try being nice and see what happens. She could be keen to change. And if she is, I reckon I can at least figure out a way to involve her in our lives again. In a way that'll avoid a custody battle. Because if I really am not Mia's father, we all know who'll be the victor on that one: Mia. She would probably piss off to another state. I wouldn't blame her. But even if we do work something out, that still won't change the fact that I'm in love with Sonia. And there's nothing Celeste can ever do to split us up.

I touch Celeste's hand. "Please, don't cry."

Celeste wipes her eyes with her chiffon scarf.

"I'm seeing someone. It's over between you and me. It's been over since you remarried. I thought you had moved on."

Celeste nods over and over.

"Oh, Nash, I'm sure she'll understand."

I draw my hand away. "What?"

"People leave their lovers all the time. She'll understand that you still love your wife."

I scoff. "Ex-wife. And I don't still love you."

Celeste smiles, sighs, and gulps down the last of her latté. She leans forwards and pats both my hands with hers. "I'm so glad we had this talk. I'll be in touch, okay?" Celeste stands and clutches her handbag to her chest.

I stand up too. My chair scrapes and echoes through the café. "What the fuck? What do you mean? Where are you going?" My questions fire at her like bullets.

"To visit Mia, of course."

"No, no, no. You can't. And she's at school anyway. Studying for an exam." She's not, but I don't know what else to say.

Celeste smirks like she knows I'm grasping at straws. "I'll take her out for dinner, then."

I step backwards slightly, accidentally knocking my chair over. It hits the floor with a clang, and everybody in the café falls silent. But I don't give a shit. I can't let Celeste get to Mia and tell her I'm not her dad. This is nuts.

Why is she doing this to me?

"Celeste!" I grab her arm. "Stop. Leave Mia alone. She's not ready."

Celeste yanks her arm away from me, frowns, and glares. She's lost it. What did Karter *do* to her?

"Sir!" calls a waiter, and sprints to our side. "We will not tolerate this behaviour on our premises. Please leave."

"Me? Leave?" I yell. "I'm not the problem here. It's her."
I poke Celeste between her breasts and she stumbles backwards melodramatically.

"I don't know about that, sir." The waiter puts his hands on his hips and gestures towards the exit with his eyebrows.

"It's okay." Celeste composes herself, flutters her eyelids, and pushes her tits out. "We were just having a slight disagreement. We're both leaving now, anyway." She smiles and hooks her arm around my elbow. "Don't forget your wallet, darling."

I take a deep breath, pick up my wallet and keys, and escort Celeste out of the café. With Celeste still on my arm, we walk silently to my car. My mouth goes dry and my throat is scratchy. I don't know how to get out of this mess.

We reach my car and I remove Celeste's arm from mine, unlock the driver's seat door, and stand behind it. The only way I'm going to get her to do what I want is if I act vulnerable. It's obvious that this is some sort of power trip. She has always shown traits of being a control freak, especially with keeping Mia fit, but it seems that now it's well and truly reared its ugly head. She's obsessive.

"Please don't go to see Mia. She doesn't know you're here," I say slowly, as if Celeste's recent past seems to have sucked all the intelligence from her brain.

"Why not?" Celeste says. Calm. She tilts her head to the side. I watch thoughts of her next manipulative remark flicker behind her eyes.

"Because I don't want you to say anything yet. For her.

She's having a tough time—at school. It won't be good for her right now."

"Why? Because she might bury her sorrows in junk food?"

I frown and crane my neck inward. "Come again?"

"You know what I'm talking about."

"She told you?"

"She didn't have to. I'm her mother. Mothers just know." Celeste taps her nose.

"You hardly speak to her."

"I know. Trust me."

"You lost that privilege a long time ago."

"Believe what you want to believe, Nash. And relax." She sucks her cheeks in and traces her right eyebrow with the nail of her forefinger. "Fine. I won't say anything to her. The last thing I need is a daughter who is even more overweight than she already is. I'll wait until we're all together again."

I scratch my beard, tap the top of the car door, and gaze down the street. "I s'pose I'm going to have to take your word for it."

"Fabulous. When would you like to do dinner?"

I laugh and shake my head. "You don't get it, do you?"

"What is there to get?"

"I don't want you back."

Celeste's fake possessed-looking grin surfaces again. She slowly scrapes a sharp pointy nail down my cheek and says, "Yes. You do." She squeezes my cheeks together with one hand and pulls me closer like she's about to kiss me.

But she doesn't.

She whispers, "I'm staying at the Hilton. Expect a call."

chapter 93

mia
i think he caught me

I sit on the sofa. Turn on my iPod and scroll through all the Magic Dirt tracks. I press play on "Dirty Jeans" and rhythmically hit the side of my head on the wall to its 4/4 beat. A lawn mower spits into action next door. I turn the volume up. Bite the side of my tongue with my molars and wonder if I've still got any chocolate hidden in my room.

I realize it's the first time I've thought about food in a week. Ever since I started thinking about Mick.

Kimi. Football field.

Revenge. Murder.

I burp in disgust, stop the head thump, and try to reach for my toes. I smile when I realize I can now reach a little further past my knees. And I'm not even trying that hard. I'd cut out the sugar and the booze. And voila!

The bright blue light from my mobile phone flashes just as the song launches into the chorus: "You're an ordinary boy, and that's the way I like it . . ." I yank the headphones from my ears and pick it up. It's Dad.

"Hey."

"Where are you?" He's panting.

"Where are *you*?"

"You home?"

"Yeah . . . what's—"

"Are you okay?" Dad takes a deep breath.

"Yes. Are *you*?"

Dad sighs and laughs as if he's just heard a joke. "Yeah."

"That's uh, great then, Dad."

"Yep. Look, what are you doing for dinner?"

I get up and look at my reflection in a picture frame. Picture frames are better than mirrors because you can't see too much detail. I like that black kohl around my eyes makes me look gangsterish. I smile.

"Salad?"

"Again? But you're doing so great. You should reward yourself. Let's go out. Let's go to that place on the other side of town you like. You know, the one with all the S&M stuff all over the walls."

Dad speaks so fast I can hardly recognize where his sentences are meant to begin or end.

"Who said I like S&M shit?" Is he for real?

Dad pauses. His breathing is all erratic. Maybe he's rubbing his beard. Or maybe he's holding the phone to his chest. Or something. What the hell?

"Oh, maybe that was Sonia."

"Uh . . . TMI, Dad!" Oh my God. He didn't just tell me that. I squeeze my eyes shut trying to erase the image.

"Sorry, uh, don't worry about it. How about the Docklands?"

"Dad, you're freaking me out."

More silence.

"Are you sure you're okay, Mia?"

"Why do you keep asking me that?"

Long pause.

"Because I'm your father."

"And?"

"Be ready at seven. I'm taking you out."

"Okay, but—"

I finish my sentence to beeping. I put my phone down and frown at my reflection. And then it hits me.

Shit. He knows about the drugs. I'm screwed.

chapter 99

sonia

$$\varphi = \frac{1 + \sqrt{5}}{2} = 1.6180339887 \ldots$$

I step into the staff room to retrieve my belongings. Nash is at his desk. Why is he back here? I notice relief on his face as he hangs up his phone. I don't want to talk to him. I can't talk to him. Maybe I can quickly grab my handbag without making any noise. He hasn't seen me yet. I need to escape having to look into his eyes, into the soul I will have to constantly lie to until I decide how I'm going to incarcerate Ibrahim. The longer Ibrahim is a threat to my family, the longer I will be a threat to myself and everyone I love. And if Mick loses me, he'll become just like his father. I cannot let that happen. He deserves a real future.

I can't let Nash get involved in this either. I promised him I had stopped. And I don't want to lose him. He is the only one holding me together right now.

Luckily all he knows is that I suspect Ibrahim is back in town. I can't let him know it's a fact. If Nash knows he's here, he won't be able to control himself. Ibrahim will pull him in. And that would be dangerous. For everybody. Nash had a hard enough time escaping Ibrahim's sly manipulation the first time.

As far as Nash is concerned, it's only Mick that might

be involved with Ibrahim. And it has to stay that way. He's worried enough as it is about the fiasco with Mia and Celeste. Imagine having to find out that I'm dragging his daughter into this mess too?

My heart beats heavily in my ears at the thought.

I tiptoe to my desk. Just as I lift up my bag, my mobile phone rings. Darn it. Nash flicks his head around. He smiles, looking a little confused. I drop into my seat and hang my head in my hands.

Nash walks over to me and rubs my shoulders. He smells like he's had a rigorous game of football with sweaty teens. He digs his thumbs between my shoulder blades. I sit up straight and roll my head from side to side.

"You're so tense. Tough classes today?" Nash moves his thumbs up to the base of my head. The crunch of my hair against my scalp reminds me of death. I flick Nash's hand away.

I anticipate the question. I know it's coming. Maybe I should prepare answers for all the possible questions Nash could ask from here on in. This isn't going to be an easy ride.

Hell, has any of my life been an easy ride?

"So, how's it all going at home? Have you gotten to the bottom of anything yet?" he says.

I spin around in my chair, smile, nod enough for it to be considered a yes but also mistaken for the mere acknowledgment of the question. That will give me a few more moments to figure out a response.

I swallow. Sigh.

Nash frowns and nods as if nudging me to speak. I can hear his brain ticking, thinking, *What's gotten into you?*

"Fine. Sorted." I realize I sound like Nash and offer a crooked smile. I use Nash's arm to pull myself up and hook my handbag over my shoulder.

"Shit, Sonia, that's great."

"Yes. It is."

Is he going to push it, or is he going to get the hint that I'm not feeling very talkative?

"What's wrong?"

"Nothing. I said everything is fine."

"Doesn't look like it."

"Can we just get going?" I purse my lips and squint at a fleck of ash stuck in Nash's beard. His eyes are slightly red. Like he's been crying.

He smiles, brushes hair from my eyes, and cups my cheek. "You'd tell me if it was serious?"

I nod and withdraw, clutching the handle of my handbag so tight the tips of my fingers sting. I release my grip and vertically straighten my arms.

"I'm sorry. I really need to get a move on."

Nash frowns and steps forwards. He reaches out and gently touches my elbow. "Wait. Don't you have detention duty?"

I smack my forehead into my palm. "Fuck."

"Wow." Nash laughs.

I forgot I haven't sworn in front of him for ages.

"If you've got somewhere to be, I can cover for you," Nash says.

"You don't have plans?"

"None that can't wait an hour."

I peck Nash on the cheek and dash to my car without uttering another word.

Mick and I need to figure out our next move.

chapter 45

mia
s&m? really, dad?

Dark. Purple. Random crystals hanging from the ceiling. This restaurant reminds me of *Moulin Rouge*. Any moment now Nicole Kidman is going squeal and flash her frilly crotch.

"Why here?" I say. How does he know about this creepy place?

Dad shrugs, unfolds his napkin, and lays it on his lap.

"And what's going on? You were fucking weird on the phone this afternoon."

"I wasn't acting weird. And can you watch your mouth, please? In public at least?"

I take a deep breath, puff up my cheeks, and look at the menu. It's covered in red and silver glitter, and it sticks to my fingers. Reminds me of kindergarten. I hold my hand out to show Dad. "Think I'll be shitting shinies by the end of the night?" I giggle.

Dad laughs through his nose, scratches his chin, but doesn't look up from his menu. "Porterhouse Steak for me. Know what you're having?" Dad turns his head towards the bar. Glitter glistens in his beard. I smile. He looks so sweet and gentle. I realize how much I love him, how much he's been trying to be supportive, and how much I've been pushing him away. I feel a little sick in the stomach thinking about the way I've been treating him. Especially when I spat at him. That totally wasn't me. I was wasted. And now I regret it so bad.

"What?" Dad laughs, as if my staring has made him nervous.

I open my eyes wide and shake my head.

A waitress approaches our table wearing a slightly see-through white bead-encrusted blouse with a bright-purple bra underneath. I want to laugh. But I control myself. I wonder if she's trying to fit in with the decor, or if the owner of the place has made her dress like this. In which case, I guess I'd better not judge.

Dad glances up from his menu, notices the waitress's blouse, and quickly looks down again.

"Ahem. I'll uh . . . uh . . . I'll have the Porterhouse Steak, medium rare, thanks."

The waitress nods and pushes her crotch into the edge of the table. I internally gag. She looks at me with a flashy white smile—a wordless request to take my order.

"Chef's salad," I say, focusing on Dad's beard.

"Mia, come on. Treat yourself today. We should celebrate."

I frown. "What are we celebrating?"

"Your awesome effort in los—"

"Dad. TMI?"

"Oh—" Dad hides his mouth with the menu and whispers, "To lose weight."

I roll my eyes, look at the waitress, and mimic her smile. "Chef's salad, thanks."

"Sweet. Ya-wan-anythin'-ta-drink?"

Dad and I exchange glances and say in unison, "Carlton Draught Light."

"Won't-be-long. I'll-bring-ya-beers-in-a-sec." The waitress takes the menus. The flop of her thongs reverberates across the wooden floor.

"So," Dad says, combing his fingers through his hair and making the front of it stick up like a cockatoo, "you've been spending a lot of time with Mick lately."

I look into my lap. "Yeah. So?" I say a bit too defensively. I knew he had an ulterior motive for taking me out.

"I think it's good, that's all."

Silence. We both seem to be waiting for the other to say something.

"What?" I tense up. Is he onto me? He couldn't be, could he? And even if he was, I've stopped. So he wouldn't be able to prove it. But what if Sonia says something to him? Nah. That would never happen. She'd risk too much. And then Dad'd blame Mick. For everything. And then their relationship would be over. And that would suck. Because Dad's happy with Sonia. She's good for him. Even if she is a bit weird sometimes. And seriously? Mick's so much nicer than he makes out. If only he would try to speak better, more people would like him. I'm sure of it. It's all the "fuck this fuck that, cunt, blah blah blah." I guess, though, it's his toughness that first attracted me to him. So maybe I shouldn't be complaining.

Dad rearranges the cutlery on the table, then puts it back where it was, takes a deep breath, holds it in, then exhales with a heavy sigh.

"Actually, we need to talk."

Here we go. I knew it. I brace myself.

"Before it gets out of hand—" Dad squeezes his eyes shut for a moment, and it seems like he's banging his fists on his knees under the table. "Wait. Promise me something first—"

Oh no, he does know!

"Dad, seriously, you don't have to be worried. It was just a phase. I promise. I've stopped."

Dad frowns and cranes his neck.

"Phase? Stopped?"

"Yeah, I mean, it was stupid. I know it was stupid. I knew it was really fucking stupid, but I really hated myself, you know? The way I look? I mean, who would like the way I look, right? But then, you know, Mick, he's cool. And he made me realize something."

Dad slowly leans back into his seat and scratches his beard. "Okay. I'm sorry. We're not on the same page."

What? Shit!

"Uh—" I squash my hands between my knees and look away.

"I'm glad, though. That you stopped," Dad says. "I knew you would. Eventually. I trusted you to figure it out for yourself."

I look up. "You *knew*?"

"Yep."

"And you never tried to stop me?"

"Thought about it."

"So why didn't you?"

Sadness fills Dad's eyes. "I didn't want to push you away any more than I already had."

That's my fault. I'm the one who made him feel like that. How could I have been so horrible to him when all he ever does is do the best he can for me? "Dad, I would never—"

"Here-ya-are-two-Carlton-Draught-Lights-Yer-meals-won't-be-long." The waitress slaps our beers on the table so hard it makes the table shake and suds spill everywhere. She puts her hands on her hips and flashes her toothpaste-commercial grin at us again.

Dad smiles in thanks.

The waitress spins around on one foot and walks to the bar, thongs flapping on the soles of her grimy cracked heels. She sits on a bar stool, rolls her eyes, pulls a piece of chewing gum off the bar surface, and sucks it into her mouth.

"Man," I say. "Really, who told you about this place?"

"Promise you won't laugh?"

"I won't."

"Sonia and I come here sometimes."

"Right." I say, mockingly dragging out the word.

"Can I ask you a question?"

I sip my beer and nod. My teeth clang against the glass—it sends a nerve pain through my jaw. Ow.

"Seeing as you've been spending time with Mick, have you noticed anything weird about Sonia lately?"

I lower my pint and wipe my mouth with the back of my hand. For some reason I don't think that this is what he wanted to speak to me about.

I flatten my lips together and shake my head. This is not good. Not a good question at all. He can't even be suspicious. Because if he is, he could get himself caught up in some crazy shit. And Sonia made it very clear that it wasn't in his best interests. And he's been to hell and back with Mum already. He couldn't cope being betrayed again, she said.

I have to protect him from this. As much as I possibly can.

"No? She seemed a bit wired at work."

"Haven't noticed." I shake my head again and look at the waitress sitting at the bar. I have to change the subject. I try to make him laugh by mimicking the waitress's speech "I'm-hungry-are-you-hungry?-You-think-our-food-will-be-long?"

Dad smiles with suspicion in his eyes.

Pretty sure he knows I'm trying to distract him. Why why why? Please, Dad. Just drop it. Let's enjoy this dinner together. Let's forget the world and the shit and the fucked-up people in it and pretend we are the only ones left. Because him, sitting here, in front of me tonight, it's nice. I miss . . . us.

I want to tell him how much I love him.

I want to tell him how much I appreciate all the times he cooked me healthy meals even though he was dying to order pizza and drink beer.

I want to tell him how much I appreciate him fobbing Mum off every time she called to speak to me.

I want him to know that I'll never forget the day he risked his job by giving one of the dudes in his PE class a detention for no reason because he bullied me about my weight.

But all I can muster is touching his hand and saying, "Don't worry, Dad. I think you're just being paranoid."

And I swear to God, I feel like my heart skips a beat.

chapter 96

mick

sometimes *fuck* means a lotta shit

I gotta thank Mia for clearin' the air between Mum 'n' me. I've never felt so at fuckin' ease with 'er before. It's like I've just hooked up with a mate I haven't seen in ages or somethin'. I was so fuckin' stupid to keep this shit with Dad a secret from 'er. She's the one with the fuckin' experience in this shit. But she was tryin' so hard, ya know? It hurt deep inside me chest to think that I'd be the one to ruin that for 'er.

Fuck it. I guess this is for the best. Once ya see the blood, it's in ya blood. There's no escapin'.

Mum 'n' me sit on the back porch 'n' share a smoke. She don't do it much. But sometimes she says she jus' likes to chill with one. She takes a real long drag 'n' then passes it to me.

"I have an idea," Mum says, blowin' the smoke towards the sky 'n' then turnin' to face me. "But I need you to approve it first."

I frown 'n' rub me hands up 'n' down me knees. "Me? Why me?" I laugh. She's gotta be kiddin'. "You're the old-time pro with all this shit."

Mum screws up her mouth 'n' nods, "Well, I can't help

thinking that we could somehow use Kimi as bait to get Ibrahim caught."

"What the fuck, Mum? You have a fuckin' death wish for 'er, or somethin'?"

"No, I'm serious. We could do this. Here's what I'm thinking." Mum grabs the smoke off me, sucks in the last bit, drops it on the step, 'n' butts it out with 'er foot.

"Kimi needs money. That's the whole reason she's doing this funny business with Mia and trying to get your knives. What if we approach her and offer her a bit more cash than what she could earn by selling them, to lure Ibrahim here?"

I look at 'er. Like she's off 'er fuckin' rocker. But it's genius.

"We could anonymously tip off Narcotics. Tell them that Ibrahim is going to turn up at such and such a time. They wouldn't ignore it."

I shake me head.

"It would be the best arrest they'd made in decades. They've been after him since you were born. Did you know that?" Mum stares at me 'n' hooks 'er feet under 'er bum, sits like a li'l girl on the floor of a classroom. I didn't know that. I hardly know nothin' about me parents. All I know is that every time they went out, someone came back with blood on their clothes. Or skin. I used to think it was me mum's blood. From Dad hittin' 'er. But I'm startin' to think it wasn't hers at all. Ever.

"We can use her as bait, Mick. She can make it so Ibrahim 'accidentally' sees her steal something from his office,"

Mum says, doin' those quote things with 'er fingers. "And walk out the door with it, then head to a pickup point, collect a brick of cocaine, and bring it here. You know your dad. There's no way he'd stop her in the middle of it. He'd follow her. The thrill is in the catch. Forever and always. And he'd want to make her suffer for it."

I take a deep breath 'n' shake me head. "Mum, it's too fuckin' dangerous. Not only for us, but there's no way Kimi's gonna do that. Mia said she's shit scared of 'im. And anyway, how would it work? How's she gonna get the coke without gettin' hold of the knives to sell first? Dad's been trying to get me to trade 'em for it."

"That's not the point of the weapons, Mick. He's just testing you. He wants you to know how it feels to be under pressure. He's training you. It's what he did to me. He has all the cocaine in the world. He doesn't need you to get cocaine for him; he needs you to show him that you *can* get cocaine for him, that with the right motivation you would put yourself in danger to get a job done no matter the consequence. Anyway, just leave that part to me."

I think 'bout what she jus' said for a minute. I'm such a dick for not gettin' that Dad was tryin' to train me up. And then it hits me. Why does Mum wanna try 'n' trap Dad again if he's not gonna try 'n' kill 'er? What's the point of all of it? Is she doin' this for me?

"Whaddaya gonna do?" I say.

"I still have connections, you know. You really think after being with Ibrahim for twenty years, I didn't learn the tricks of the trade?" Mum laughs.

I swallow. Jesus fuckin' Christ. She really wants to go through with this?

"Mum, you're totally fucked up, you know that?"

Mum smiles 'n' raises her eyebrows. "Thanks?"

"I jus' got one question." I cough and spit between me feet. "Where you gonna get the dough to give Kimi?"

"Come on, Mick. Just because I don't say anything, doesn't mean I don't know it."

I frown at her. "You gotta be so fuckin' cryptic?"

"*You*," Mum says, poking me in the chest, "have more than enough money to help with that."

I think I blush. I thought she didn't know.

"Awright," I say, rubbin' me hands over me head. "But even if we did do this shit, what comes next? I mean, fuck. Even if narcs do nab 'im walkin' outta here with that amount of drugs, Dad'll have his men onta ya—onta us—in no time 'n' we'll be totally fucked. And anyway, how ya gonna find out where to send Kimi to get it?"

Mum looks at the row of magpies sittin' all peaceful along the back fence.

"I know what I'm doing," she says. "You just need to trust me. Do you trust me?"

"Do I 'ave a choice?"

Mum smiles 'n' rests a hand on me shoulder.

"Not really."

"Awright. When do we do it?"

"Friday. Let's set it up for this Friday. Night."

chapter 97

sonia

round and round the garden,
like a teddy bear ...

I flip through an old photo album looking for the Polaroid of Ibrahim standing out in front of Gaz's place with Nash. Though Ibrahim graciously let Gaz loose after Gaz became a paraplegic as a result of a job gone wrong, he might still have the connections I need to find out where Ibrahim manufactures his cocaine now.

Gaz used to live above a café, so the shop front window is bound to be in the picture. If I can find the name of the café, I can find Gaz, and hopefully tell Kimi where and how to get hold of the drugs. I can lie; I can say that she's in debt and needs a financial boost. He'd do me the favour. Surely. Especially since I kept the fact that he tried to hit on me one night all those years ago from Ibrahim. If Ibrahim had have found out about that, Gaz would have become a bloodstain on our back porch too. And I'd have been given the honours.

I dial Nash to try to calm my nerves, and hook the phone between my shoulder and ear to continue flipping through the album.

"Yello?"

"Did you tell her?"

"I tried." Nash groans. "But she thought I was talking about the drugs. And then I saw the look in her eyes, and I couldn't go through with it."

"What drugs?" I suck in my breath, trying to sound as calm as possible.

"For a mathematician, you have a very short memory."

I close my eyes. *Of course.*

"Oh. Right. Yes. Sorry, I've got a lot on my mind."

"I noticed. Do you want to talk?"

"Not really. Do you mind? Just tell me about Mia. That's she's okay. I just need to know she's okay."

There's a long pause on the other end of the line. I have to control the urgency in my voice. It's way too suspicious. "I just care about her. And you."

The guilt of dragging Mia into this is eating away at my heart more than I thought it would. I guess my self-inflicted rehabilitation has actually started to kick in. What kind of person am I? I don't even know where I stand anymore. Am I like Ibrahim, or not? Can I ever *not* be like him?

There is an end in sight, though, for the greater good. And that's the only thing I have to keep telling myself to justify my actions.

It's for the greater good.

It's for the greater good.

It's for the greater good.

"Yeah, I get it," Nash says. "She's fine. She quit. I think. She's a good kid."

"Good." I sigh. "Yeah. She's a good kid." I shake my head

at myself. I feel sick to my stomach. Mick can handle this. He's lived in the aftermath of chaos his whole life. But Mia? I have to protect her.

Silence.

"Celeste is in town."

"What? Since when?"

"Don't know. Met up with her yesterday. It was weird."

"Weird?"

"Yeah. Weird."

I scoff. "I don't know what that means, Nash."

I can hear a muffling sound as if Nash is switching the receiver to his other ear.

"Let's just say I'm not sure what's going to happen next. It seems she's going to hold off on telling Mia I'm not her father. But I don't understand why. I think you're right. It isn't true. She seems so desperate to see Mia, but she hasn't. Yet. I don't get it. To be honest"—Nash laughs— "she might need to be hospitalized. She seemed so—"

"Weird?"

"Yeah. And psychotic."

"What are you going to do?"

"Wait and see, I s'pose. I don't want to tell Mia unless I have to. I'm going to wait it out. Maybe Celeste will leave. When she gets bored."

"Weird." I smirk.

"You can say that again."

I flip over another page in the photo album and spot the photo I've been searching for. It's Ibrahim, Nash, and Gaz in their football gear after a match. And the shop front says "Martha's Bakery."

"Nash, can I call you back later? I have so much laundry to sort out, and I don't think I have any clean underwear for tomorrow."

"No worries. Wanna go out for dinner this Fri?"

Shit! This Friday? How am I going to keep them away this Friday?

"Actually," I say. *Think think think!* "I have a better idea."

"Sure, anything you like."

"Maybe you should take Mia away for the weekend. Spend some quality time together. You know, before anything changes because of Celeste. Give Mia some positive memories, you know? Recent ones. It might help keep you both solid."

"Nice idea. But I can't afford that right now."

"I'll lend you some money. Come on, it'll be really good for you both."

Please please please.

"Maybe. I'll see how I feel when the weekend rocks around. It *is* a good idea."

I clench my fists and grit my teeth. A "maybe" will have to do for now. I loosen my jaw and move it left and right.

"Okay," I say with a forced smile in my voice. "Think about it. But you'll let me know if you decide to go, won't you?"

"Sure. Why?"

Good question. Luckily I am trained to think on my feet.

"Well, you've got to tell someone, don't you? What if you have a car crash and no one knows where to look?"

Nash laughs. "Right. Thanks, Mum."

I smile and sigh with relief.

Let the games begin.

chapter 98

mick

my innards are mushy, awright?

The hard fuckin' part about wagging class is timin' it so it doesn't clash with the dicks in PE. At every corner of the fuckin' school grounds is a football field, tennis 'n' basketball court, 'n' a mini track. And yeah, there are only a few safe places to smoke too—like behind the stinkin' toilet block.

They really make teens feel like filth, ya know? Like 'cause they're under eighteen they don't have fuckin' brains. I've got fuckin' brains. I jus' like to keep 'em to meself. I don't need no one knowing I knows what everyone's thinkin'. I don't need no one knowin' shit about me either. If they wanna think I'm thick, then it's their fuckin' shit-for-brains problem. Just wait. Wait till they rub me the wrong way. Then they'll see what thick *really* fuckin' looks like.

"She's waiting for me in the football field," Mia says, snatchin' me smoke and taking the last drag.

"I should come with ya." I lean me shoulder against the graffitied wall 'n' stare at the butt Mia dropped on the ground. "You should step on that, babe."

Mia squints at me. I smirk back 'n' step on the butt meself. So what if I actually care about the planet? I've seen enough shit on TV to convince meself that I should. I'm not total loser, you know. I jus', you know, got a reputation to protect. I can't have people knowin' my innards are mushy, awright?

Mia crosses 'er arms over 'er chest 'n' sighs. "I'm not sure you coming with me is gonna help, babe. She might just freak at the first sight of you and split."

"Butcha can't do this on your own."

"Sure I can. Why can't I?"

"Ya really think she's gonna trust what ya have to say without me bein' there to prove I know?"

Mia shrugs 'n' scrunches up 'er nose. "I guess not."

I cup me hand over Mia's cheek 'n' stroke me thumb along her cheekbone.

God, she's fuckin' gorge.

I don't give a toss if she's got some skin to grab, or if she's skinny, anorexic, or even a fuckin' skeleton. With eyes like hers she's gonna *mesmerize*—is that a word?—me for as long as I'm alive 'n' can say to all the fucked-up prissy cunts in this school, "Eat shit 'n' die, bitches." And she's not even that fat anyway. She looks better than she used to when she was a fuckin' cock tease. More real. More woman. More arse. I might even love her as much as I would me own sister . . . no . . . wait . . . I wouldn't fuck me sister.

Mia leans her face into me hand and kisses me palm. Her lips feel like wet cotton wool.

"Look. Why don'tcha go first," I say. "Tell her I'm in on it 'n' explain why. And if she freaks or runs off, message me to come. I'll sort it."

Mia nods 'n' leans into me for a hug. It takes a sec for me to hug 'er back. But fuck, that's not 'cause I don't wanna. It's jus'—I can't really believe this is all for real, ya know?

A year ago, Mia was jus' like all the other chicks. Hot *as*. A bitchy slut, yeah, but still, there was somethin' funny about 'er. Not *funny* funny. Just not . . . normal.

There was somethin' in her face that called out to me.

It said: "Everythin' hurts."

And I said back: "I know."

Mia looks up 'n' kisses me on me chin. "What time is it? Should I go?"

"Prob'ly," I say, 'n' kiss 'er back on the forehead.

"Uh—I have something to tell you first." Mia pulls back. She has tears in her eyes. What the fuck? Did I do somethin'?

"I really really *really* like you," she says. "And I don't wanna lie to you. I don't want you to lie to me either, and I want this—us—to be—"

"Real?"

Mia smiles 'n' blushes a little. "Yeah. Real."

I reach out to pull her closer, but she flicks away me hand. Girls are fuckin' weird. I thought this was a "moment," and she flicks away me hand?

"Wait," she says. "You need to hear what I have to say first."

I take a deep breath. It sounds serious. I can feel me nostrils flair.

"I kinda . . . uh, fingered Kimi in the footy field the other day."

I frown 'n' then laugh. "You were trying to get shit out of her, though, right? I thought you might do somethin' like that. Smart." I nod. She's a bloody genius. I knew she had good stuff in 'er head.

"Yeah, but see, here's the thing. I—I sorta, uh—liked it?"

Fuck me! That's a man's fuckin' dream come true. What's she all wimpin' out on me for? I laugh 'n' finally manage to pull Mia into me arms. I kiss her tiny nose.

"So?" I say.

"You're not mad?" Mia's voice goes up at the end like a li'l girl's.

"Fuck off, babe. Why would I be mad?"

"Isn't it a bit weird?" Mia rests her head on me chest.

"Mia. I don't give a fuck if yer bi, or whatever it makes ya."

"Really?"

"Really." I press Mia's head inta the crook of me neck. She wraps her arms around me waist. I can feel her smilin' against me skin. "And thank you."

"I couldn't *not* tell you," Mia mumbles.

"Nah, not for that. Fuck. For helpin' my mum 'n' me with this bullshit."

Mia pulls away 'n' looks into me eyes. She smiles 'n' nods. She doesn't have to say nothin'. 'Cause I can tell that this is for real.

Mia.

My li'l creature.

I'm gonna keep 'er.

Forever and a day.

chapter 49

mia

rust—all it takes is losing a bit of trust

When I approach Kimi in the footy field she is sunbathing with earphones in again. Her skirt is hitched under the elastic of her knickers and her T-shirt below the wire of her bra.

"Hey." I poke her in the side with my toes and hover over her with my hands on my hips, trying not to think about the sex. I've got to focus on Mick now. He's the one I really want. And with him, everything is gonna be special. I just know it.

Kimi yanks the earphones out, shades her eyes from the sun, and sits upright with a grin when she sees it's me.

"Hey, yourself. I knew you'd come." Kimi makes movements to stand up, but I hold my hand out to suggest she stay where she is. The less easy it is for her to run off, the better.

"Don't get up." I kneel and sit on the lawn next to her. "I have something important I want to talk to you about."

"If it's about the other day, I—"

"It's not."

Kimi nods. "This sounds serious. Are you okay?"

"Actually, I'm great. And the reason has to do with you,"

I say. Kimi smirks as if she thinks I might be in love with her. "But can you promise me something first?"

"Sure." Kimi gently touches my knee. I look at her hand, but don't move it away even though I want to.

"I have a proposition for you. Something that is probably the answer to your prayers."

"Oh?"

"Yeah. You see, I've spoken to Mick."

"About—?" Kimi stretches the word out and lowers her head in question. I was actually expecting her to flip out at the mention of his name. But maybe she was expecting my idea to involve Mick all along. I shouldn't be so quick to judge a person's intelligence. Which means right now I also need to be really careful this goes exactly to plan. I can't let Sonia and Mick down. Not just because I think I'm in love with Mick but because it would be letting Dad down too. If what Sonia said to me is true, that Dad promised Ibrahim he'd never interfere with his business in exchange for Ibrahim never asking Dad for any favours, then the plan *has* to work. Because if it doesn't, Ibrahim will find out about Sonia and Dad seeing each other, and then everything would turn to shit. For all of us.

Because, obviously, Ibrahim would just assume that Dad was in on all this.

"I've come to talk about your . . . predicament."

"What the fuck, Mia?" Kimi yells. "Do you have any idea how much trouble this is gonna get me in? You have no idea who Daddy really is! He's gonna flip—"

Kimi stands up, but I grab her skirt and yank her back down. This, I was definitely expecting. And I'm prepared for it. Kimi lands on the grass with a thud.

"Kimi, just hear me out. I *know* who he is. And I had a feeling you knew too. I knew you were hiding something, and I *know* you're not a bad person. And you know what else I know?" I say this all as quickly as possible while trying not to sound like a lunatic.

Kimi sniffs and shakes her head. A tear rolls down her cheek.

"I know how to help you. *We* know how to help you. And it involves you getting enough money to leave Thornbury and start fresh in another city. Country even."

"We?" Kimi's eyes open wide in disbelief.

"Me and Mick." Kimi looks at me as if I'm insane. "And Mrs. Shâd."

"His *mother*? Are you out of your freaking mind?"

"No, actually. Do you want the money or not?"

Kimi turns her head and looks towards the road. The neighbourhood is quiet this afternoon. Kimi wipes her eyes really quickly with the heels of her hands.

"How much are we talking?" she says.

"Fifty grand. Half today, half after the job is done."

"Jesus Christ, fifty grand?" Kimi speaks way too loudly, but then drops her volume midsentence.

I nod.

"Sign me up. What do I have to do?" Kimi takes a deep shaky breath.

"Mrs. Shâd has organized an afterschool 'maths tutorial' for you. Meet her in the Maths and Sciences Wing, room A5 at 3:30. She'll give you the 25k—cash—and tell you what needs to be done."

Kimi smiles as if she's just inhaled laughing gas, but it disappears just as fast.

"I'm not killing anyone."

I laugh. "It's a lot tamer than that." I shock myself at how calm I am while saying all of this. But the good thing is, it will all be over really soon, and life can go back to normal. Dad and Sonia don't have to be scared of Ibrahim anymore, and me and Mick don't have to worry about our parents ending up dead.

She stares at me. Her eyes glisten. "Is this all some ploy to get rid of me?"

"Of course not. Why would I want to get rid of you?"

"I dunno. Everybody wants to get rid of me." Kimi bursts into tears.

I should have known she was insecure. Just like Mick, it's all show. That toughness, that withdrawal from society—well, if you can call the students at school a society. I guess it is kinda.

"This will really help you," I say. "You can start a new life. Be anyone and anything you like. It's a chance to be a good person. Do things right this time."

Kimi wails and falls into my arms. I hug her tight, and she shakes up and down in my embrace. Her tears smear against my cheek. They're warm and somehow remind me of the day my mum left. I cried for so long in Dad's lap that I gave myself a headache. My mascara stained his jeans. When I apologized for making such a mess of them, he stroked my hair and said, "You can cry on me as much as you like, and your tears will never stain me." I didn't get it then. But I think I do now. I think he meant that no matter what happens, he will always love me.

Kimi doesn't have anyone in her life to love her.

My dislike for her turns to pity. And I can only wish this deal with Sonia does actually do her some good. But for some reason, seeing her like this, sitting here, witnessing her cry for the first time, in this silent football field where my dad and Ibrahim once kicked for the same team, I'm suddenly worried.

About Kimi, about Sonia, about Dad.

About Mick.

I swallow. And say something that makes the hairs on my arms stand on end.

"Trust me," I say as I stroke Kimi's hair. "Everything is gonna turn out for the best."

chapter 50

sonia
kimiko is a go-go

I sit at the back of the classroom with Mick's schoolbag—stuffed with twenty-five thousand dollars—between my legs. The home time bell rang fifteen minutes ago, but feet are still shuffling in through the corridor. I panic that I should have made the meeting later in case someone accidentally walked in.

I scan the room for a hiding place to put the bag until Kimiko arrives, but someone knocks on the door before I find one. My heart rate increases, and I'm shocked at the adrenaline rush. I used to be so calm in situations like this.

I leave the bag on the seat and walk to the door. My eyes are drawn to the needle of a compass on the teacher's desk as I walk by, and I envision stabbing it in someone's face to simply watch the blood run to the edge of their jaw, hang momentarily in a teardrop curve before hitting the victim's silky breast.

I peer through the blinds on the classroom door to check it's Kimiko. It is. I open it and hold my hand out to shake. She looks at my hand as though it might contaminate her with Ebola, then slips inside without touching me.

"So you're the one who broke Daddy's heart," she says in

a tone not suited to a girl her age, then sits on the teacher's desk with her knees spread.

"Firstly," I say, gently pushing her knees together, "he is not a poor man. And secondly, I didn't break his heart." I wonder why I feel the need to respond to her naive interrogation—I don't owe the girl a thing. But she's biting the inside of her bottom lip. She's clearly trying to act tough and impress me, and so I have a deep desire to set her straight. "Ibrahim's heart is unbreakable. It's made of Gorilla Glass." I smirk within while keeping my facial expression unchanged.

Kimiko's eyebrows move closer together. "Really?"

I laugh. "No. Of course not."

"Oh." She smiles a crooked smile and holds out her hand. It seems the joke did the trick. I like her. We shake hands.

"So . . . Mia says you wanna pay me fifty grand to help nab Gorilla man."

I smile at her attempt to continue the joke. It's a terrible attempt, but it's certainly a good sign. If she is so easily social, the probability of her being successful with the job is high.

"That's the gist of it, yes," I say.

"Cool. What do I have to do?"

"Well—"

"Wait. She also said you'd gimme half up front."

I raise my eyebrows.

"I wanna see it."

I'm surprised at her impatience. Impatience could be a

problem. On the other hand, it could also mean she knows what she's doing and would be hard to fool. I decide to assume the latter.

"Good call," I say. I walk to the back of the classroom and fetch the bag. I drop it in Kimiko's lap.

She sniffs it and frowns. "It smells like Mick."

I purse my lips. "Is that going to be a problem for you?"

Kimiko shrugs. "I was expecting a briefcase or something."

"This isn't a movie, Kimiko. If a girl like you was walking around with a briefcase, it would look suspicious." Perhaps I should take my last thought back.

"Oh yeah, I guess. I just thought . . . anyway, doesn't matter." She unzips the bag, peers inside, and grins. "Okay, shoot."

"Let's sit at the back."

"Why?"

I glare at her, hoping the look alone is enough explanation, otherwise I might have to reevaluate the girl's abilities.

"Okay." She jumps off the desk and walks to the back of the room as though she is rehearsing for a catwalk.

"There's a little blue notebook inside the bag. Pull it out."

She does, and she holds it in the air as though to ask if it's the correct one. Of course it's the correct one. There is nothing inside the bag but money and one notebook. My stomach tightens at the thought of her idiocy. I grit my teeth and tame the urge to call the whole thing off.

"Open it," I say with a nod. "Inside is a map of your

route, and pickup and drop-off points from where you live. Step-by-step instructions are written in there too. You can't go wrong. Read them now so I can be sure you understand it all. If you wish to ask any questions, you may ask them before you leave the classroom."

Kimiko nods and opens the book. Her expression changes from exhilaration, to surprise, to confusion, to comprehension, and last of all to worry as she reads the last instruction.

"What if he doesn't do what you say he's going to do?"

"Ibrahim is ninety-nine percent predictable to me."

"But what if he's not."

"Mick will be following you. If anything happens that is unforeseen, Mick will step in and introduce a distraction. Ibrahim will not hurt his son."

"Yeah, but—"

My throat tightens. "Do you want the money or not? Then stop being nosy and do what you're told."

Kimiko smacks her lips. "Sure, not problem. I—I got this."

"Good. Do you need anything else?"

"Nope, I'm cool." Kimiko smiles, drops the notebook in the bag, and zips it closed. "Can I go?"

I nod and reposition a pin in my hair. I watch as she walks out.

Her hair is so black and her skin is so pale and smooth. She would look brilliant in red.

chapter 51

nash

mad for marriage on a friday night

Mia is sitting on the couch entranced by a blank TV screen, clutching her mobile phone in her hand.

"Whatcha doin'?" I say. "Admiring your reflection?" I regret the comment as soon as it comes out of my mouth, but it doesn't seem to faze her. "Come on, mate, get into gear; we gotta go."

Mia snaps out of her trance and looks up. "Huh?"

"I wanna get a move on."

"To where?"

"To Sonia's?"

It could be my imagination, or the eerie orange twilight, but it looks as if Mia has jaundice. For a moment I'm taken aback by her appearance, but then she shifts her head and the light falls over it differently, and she looks normal again.

"To Sonia's? What the fuck for?" Mia says. She's swearing an awful lot lately. Mick's influence?

I glare at her. Our eyes lock. She doesn't even flinch. There's no reason for her to be behaving like this towards me. What did I do? I thought everything was okay between us again. Especially after dinner the other night. Is this some sort of drug withdrawal? I've heard of mood swings, but this looks like some form of paranoia with her knee jumping up and down like that.

"I told you. I want to surprise her." I pull a tiny crimson velvet box out of my pocket and hold it out for Mia to see. It rests in my palm like a little furry animal.

"Oh my God, Dad! Now? What happened to going away this weekend? Why aren't we going anywhere?" Mia's tone shifts from furious to enticingly calm. "It could be fun, you know."

Something isn't right. How did she know about Sonia's idea to go away? I put the box back in my pocket and scratch my beard. "Who told you that?"

Mia rolls her eyes like she does when she's been caught out. But she also has a talent to make it look like the other person's mistake.

"You, probably," she says, shrugging. Of course that would be her answer.

Let it be?

Not this time.

Christ, I'm so fed up with her mood swings. Sure, she's a teenager. But she also just inflicted herself with two weeks of brain-altering drugs. I need to put my foot down. I need to tell her to get a grip, otherwise things aren't going to be so bloody easy around here anymore.

"I didn't tell you, mate," I say with a clear firmness in my voice. "Are you listening in on my private phone conversations again? Because I've gotta say, I thought you'd grown out of that."

"Don't be ridiculous."

"I'll tell you who's being ridiculous, mate. You. Snap out of this shit and act like a supportive loving daughter for once? I do so much for you and you take it all for granted. Just once. I need you to be here for *me*. Come with me, so that I can bloody propose, before your mother—" I cut myself off and feign a cough.

Mia stands up and walks towards me. She seems oblivious to the mention of her mother. Good. I s'pose her mood swings are good for something.

She touches my shoulder, a little awkwardly, but at least it's an attempt at some affection. "I know Mum is gonna be in town soon, and you're anxious about it. I'm really sorry I don't acknowledge that it's going to be hard for you to see her again. I'm sorry I've been so fucked up. But asking Sonia to marry you isn't going to stop whatever it is you're afraid is going to happen when you see Mum."

So she wasn't oblivious, just totally and utterly mature and logical. Bloody oath. If only that was my problem, then I would probably take her advice. I nod and scratch my beard.

If only Mia knew the extent of it.

"What exactly are you afraid of, Dad? That you still have feelings for her?"

I look up and clench my jaw. Mia steps back and crosses her arms. She seems impatient. What exactly does she think she is going to achieve by keeping me here? Does she not approve of the partnership? If not, why can't she just come out and say it? And why didn't she say anything earlier?

"You wouldn't understand."

"Then why don't we chill out here tonight. I dunno, screw my diet—we can order pizza and drink beer like old times. *The Footy Show* is on tonight. We can watch that. Then you can tell me what's on your mind."

This is blatant manipulation. She sounds like Celeste.

"My feelings are not for your ears, mate. Trust me," I say.

"Jesus Christ, Dad, I'm not *two*."

I groan. What has got into her? How has she managed to make me feel like the child here?

"I don't want to fight with you. It's private. Respect that, please?"

Mia shrugs and looks at the floor.

"Good. Now we're going to Sonia's."

Mia stamps her foot and screams, "I don't want to go to Sonia's."

"If you're not two, then why are you having a two-year-old tantrum?" I yell so hard the corners of my mouth burn.

"Because—Because I think—"

I walk towards the front door. "Fuck this. I'll go on my own."

"Wait!" Mia grabs her mobile phone, bolts to the front door, and stands against it. "Just—just wait a second."

I shift the weight between my feet and huff and puff over-enthusiastically. Mia taps off a message, remaining between me and the door. She then stares at the phone until she gets the *ding* of her delivery report.

"You done?" I say, craning my neck. "I'd like to be in a good mood for my future wife."

Mia sighs, spins around, and opens the door.

"Fine. I'm coming with you."

chapter 52

celeste

it's party time

I park a couple of doors down from my old house—the smile on my face so wide that my lips feel like stretched labia in the midst of giving birth.

I never called to arrange it, like I said I would, but what the hell. What the hell! It's a surprise visit. Who doesn't like surprise visits? Everybody likes surprise visits! *Surprise!* Then everyone laughs and hugs and clinks champagne glasses, and chats all night long reminiscing about the past and getting excited about the future. *Aw!*

I'm going to traipse in, cook dinner for them all with whatever ingredients they have in the fridge—surely Mia will enjoy something other than a meat pie and tomato sauce for a change—and then take Nash aside once Mia has gone to bed like the good little girl she always is—satisfied and joyful, of course—and tell him that if he takes me back, I will never—*never ever!*—tell Mia about him not being her father. *Ha!*

I can hardly believe he fell for it. He fell for it! He's as gullible as they come. That's right. Gullible as gullible comes. I knew I could play him like Play-Doh.

But—and here's the catch—if he doesn't take me back,

he's going to be making a colossal mistake, because I won't hesitate to pull my Ruger SP101 out of my purse and subject them both to suicide.

One quick gunshot to my temple.

Over and out.

What've I got to live for anyway if I can't get my old life back?

Nothing. Nothing at all. *Nothing at all!*

I smile, wink at my purse, and jiggle in my seat.

This is perfect. *Perfect!*

Nash loves Mia more than the footy—of course he's going to choose the only way to avoid hurting her. And what a kind offer, really, offering to put a family back together again. *Yes!* I should be awarded mother of the year. *I should, I should!*

I turn off the ignition, and Nash and Mia step outside the house.

No! This is not the way it's supposed to go!

For a second I contemplate saving it for tomorrow. But stuff it. I'm all geared up for a good night out. Stuff it stuff it—stuff the chicken with weed.

I swallow another Xanax, my fifth today—and I'm still standing!—and wash it down with a swig of vodka from my tiny gold flask.

Stupid doctor. I do not have a paradoxical reaction to sedatives, thank you very much. "What utter bollocks," I say to myself in a bad British accent. "I'm just a jolly old lass!"

I drop the flask back into my bag. It lands on my handgun and clunks like a plastic bullet hitting a metal target.

I wait for Nash and Mia to turn the corner at the end of the block before starting the car again. Wherever they are headed, I am headed too.

It's time to get the party started.

As I pull away from the curb, my vision becomes a little blurred, and I misjudge the distance between the front bumper and someone's street bin. It tumbles over with a crash. A light turns on in a window. Curtains flutter. A set of eyes peek through a slit in the blinds.

I giggle and back up, correct the steering wheel, and tail Nash and Mia from a safe distance.

Tonight is going to be special. *Special!*

Tonight will, in fact, be the best night of my life.

chapter 53

mia
gotta love ya and leave ya

When Sonia answers the door, all the feeling drains from my face. My stomach sinks in sync. Sonia is wearing a vintage wedding dress and dolled up with bright-red lipstick.

I open my mouth to try to apologize for not being able to keep Dad away, but I can't stop staring.

Dad's facial expression becomes very sad. He lifts his arm to balance himself against the door frame. With his other hand he reaches towards Sonia and brushes a thick floppy lock of hair from her eyes. I look at him with my mouth agape. Why isn't he reacting to the dress? Did she know he was coming over to propose? I don't get it. Did the big Ibrahim catch already go down?

Sonia opens her mouth to speak, but nothing comes out. She moves Dad's hand away from her face instead.

"You can't be here," she says.

"Let me in. Let me help talk you through this . . . whatever it is you're going through."

Talk her through this? Talk her through *what*?

Sonia looks at her feet. And then at me as if to say, "Do something." I have to find a way for us to leave without having to give a decent reason. Should I mime illness?

Clutch over in pain? I've tried the appendix deal on Dad before—over a stupid exam. It won't work a second time. I'm out of convincing ideas.

"Sonia, you look really busy," I say. *Ugh*. "Dad, I think we should go. Sonia, I'm really sorry we just dropped in on—"

"Can you cut the crap, Mia?" Dad snaps, and squints at me, but I quickly disengage eye contact and pretend to look at something across the road.

Dad *tsks*, takes a step back, and fiddles with the box in his pocket. Something changes in his face, as if he's just caught on that Sonia and I know something he doesn't. "Can someone please tell me what's going on? That's not a question."

Sonia looks upwards, to the left. I think there is a clock on the wall. She sighs. "I've got ten minutes. Not a second more."

Nash frowns, swallows, and nods. We step inside. There's a handgun resting on the table by the door. Dad notices it and stops walking. Stares at the gun. Rubs his hands over his face and whimpers like an injured animal.

"I'll explain everything," Sonia says, with a straight face. She takes Dad's hands and leads him down the hallway. I follow. The swish of Sonia's dress as she walks is weird, and for a second I lose all sense of place. Suddenly I feel angry. Angry at Sonia, a responsible adult, for making me go through this without being able to confide in my own father. Is she really going to explain everything? If she does, then why have I been lying to Dad for so long, and feeling guilty about it, and stressed? For whom? For Mick? Or for Sonia?

"Sit." Sonia gestures for Dad to sit at the kitchen table.

He sits. I remain standing in the doorway. I don't think I can bear to look either of them in the eye right now. I clench my teeth. I just wanna get out of here before the shit goes down. So, Sonia, *please*, just tell him what's going on so that we can split and stay alive.

"Okay. I'm sitting." Dad flattens his hands on the tabletop.

"I don't have much time, so I'm just going to spit it out." Sonia stares at Dad, biting her top lip as if trying to quickly think of an excuse. She's not going to tell him the truth, is she?

Jesus Christ, Sonia. Who are you, really?

She spins around on a heel and flings open a cupboard, pulls out a few plates, and arranges them on the table. "Ibrahim is coming over for dinner, and you can't be here when he arrives."

No, no, no. Why can't she just stop pretending, man? It's over now.

I make a weird involuntary squeak of disapproval.

Sonia glares at me. I glare back.

Sonia sets the last plate in front of Dad as he cranes his neck.

"You're fucking kidding me. And why does Mia know this?"

Sonia holds her hands out, palms facing upwards. "I can't

stop my son from telling Mia about his life. I'm sorry. And I can't get out of it. You know how Ibrahim is. You don't say no to Ibrahim. And I'm sorry I didn't tell you earlier, but I didn't want you to get the wrong idea. And neither did Mia. Mick slipped up. It was a mistake. It's all a big belly-up flop."

"Bloody oath I'm getting the wrong idea, Sonia. I thought you were done with this. You promised me you were done with this shit." Dad's last couple of words push through half-closed lips.

"Look . . . it's not like that—" Sonia lifts the skirt of her dress, sits on the edge of the table, and crosses her legs. She glances at her wrist as if she's wearing a watch. She isn't. "We just need to discuss a few things. Set a few ground rules."

"In a wedding dress?"

"Yes. It will keep him subdued."

"What rules exactly?"

"Things like not entering the house in the middle of the night without my knowledge. Yada yada yada." Sonia flicks her hand as if she were uttering something unimportant.

"I thought you said Ibrahim invited himself over."

Sonia nods. "He did."

Nash laughs. "Ibrahim wanted to come over for dinner to 'discuss' something so trivial, and something he probably had no idea you knew about, and you felt the need to wear your wedding dress to subdue him."

Sonia coughs, looks up at the clock on the wall, and

wipes the sides of her mouth with her forefingers. "Well, not exactly."

"I didn't think so. Tell me what's really going on." Dad clenches his fists so hard they tremble.

"It's complicated. It's safe. I promise. But I can't talk about it."

"It's safe." Dad repeating everything Sonia says is not helping.

We need to get out of here.

Now.

Sonia puckers her brow and nods quickly, multiple times. "Uh-huh. Yes. It's safe." She shifts position of her legs, and her dress swishes again.

"I find that hard to believe," Dad says.

"I'm afraid I don't have time to wait for you to believe it, Nash. It would be better for everyone involved if you weren't here when he arrived. You especially need to get your daughter out of here."

"I thought you said it was safe," he snaps.

Dad and Sonia stare at each other for a few more moments. Neither of them flinch. Sonia reaches out and touches Dad's cheek. A tear escapes and runs down her face, hangs at the edge of her jaw.

She mouths, "I'm sorry."

Dad pushes his chair backwards and stands up. "Where's Mick?"

Sonia nods again as if she's got a twitch. "He's at the supermarket."

Dad's nostrils flare as looks around the kitchen. It's spotless. There's nothing cooking. But I swear to God, he better be finished asking questions, because the last thing we need is to get caught up in the shit that is about to go down in this house. I did my part. I helped. But being here, right now, is beginning to freak me out. A lot. It's like my organs are all huddling together to keep each other company. It's all become way too real. Especially after seeing Sonia behaving like this.

Fucking-shit-in-holy-hell-this-is-beyond-mother-fucking-fucked-up. I'll be so glad for tomorrow to come, for this to be over. Then we can all have a fresh start and move on with our lives like normal people do. I can finish school, go to Uni. Hell, I might even take that songwriting course I've had my eye on.

I bang my fist on the wall. "Dad. Let's go."

Dad looks at me with tears in his eyes.

I look at Sonia.

Sonia looks at the clock again and aggressively scratches at her elbow. Then under her chin. Then at the back of her neck.

"Nash!" Sonia screams. Tears stream down her face. "You need to leave. Right now."

Dad takes a deep breath and clenches his fists. He steps a little closer to Sonia, as if he wants to give her a hug but doesn't at the same time. But Sonia just shakes her head and cups a hand over her mouth.

"Please," she says—muffled, distant.

Dad nods and gently touches my elbow.

We walk to the front door—in silence—holding hands.

chapter 59

sonia

$$1 + 1 = 4$$

The instant Nash and Mia head towards the front door, I sniff in the snot and wipe away my tears as Kimiko bashes on the back fly wire door with a brick of cocaine.

"The White Lady is in the house!" I say, trying to act Kimi's age to make her feel more comfortable. But my attempt at relatable social interaction doesn't seem to take effect.

"I want more cash," Kimiko pants. She looks me up and down with scrutiny as she steps inside and drops the coke to the floor. It lands with a possessive thud.

"Pardon?" I shake my head. "No. We had a deal. We stick to it. Sorry." I wipe my eyes one last time. Memories of negotiations gone bad invade my thoughts.

I knew this would happen.

Negotiations never go as planned. Ever. They always want more.

"Yeah? Well, the deal changed, sistah. You have no fucking idea what I had to go through to get this. He led me on a fucking goose chase. I swear to God I thought I was gonna die by just walking through the freaking neighbourhood he stores this shit. And I could hear his footsteps. He was following my every single move. I was shitting bricks!"

"I never said it would be easy, Kimiko. You agreed to do it. A deal is a deal. So he followed you. That's what we wanted, remember? How far behind is he? You did keep track, didn't you?"

"Yeah. I'm not an idiot. He's parked right out front probably waiting to put a bullet in my head on my way out."

I frown. "That's not going to happen. You just stay in the house and you'll be safe.

"Uh . . . how?"

"What do you think I'm in a wedding dress for?"

"I have no fucking idea why you're in your stupid wedding dress."

I glare at her to suggest her sarcasm is uncalled for. "Well, in case you're interested, it's to distract him."

"Ok*aaay*."

"You wouldn't understand."

"Clearly."

The urge to slap Kimiko for her lip is rising. But I hold myself together. It's not the time or the place to get into an argument with her. "Look, go into Mick's bedroom. Lock the door. Move his dresser in front of it. Then sit in his wardrobe, inside his torture chamber thing. It'll shield you from bullets."

"What the fuck?" Kimiko shrieks.

"It's just a precaution. It won't come to that, trust me. The plan is solid. I'll come get you when it's all over."

Kimiko nods, rubbing her arms, shivering.

BOOM!

Our heads whip towards the front of the house, where screeching tyres and crashing and banging sounds barrel down the hall.

"What was that?" I whisper. My heart hovers and pounds in my throat and ears. Kimiko starts to cry.

I hesitate, hold up my hands, a gesture for Kimiko to not move yet. I turn to see if I can see what's going on outside through the edge of the living room window that's visible from where I'm standing.

Kimiko gasps.

I spin around to find a man with a fluorescent-green cap holding a hand over Kimiko's mouth and a gun to her head. Kimiko tries to struggle free by elbowing the guy in the ribs, but then her eyes widen and focus behind my head, and she starts screaming into the man's hand.

We're not the only people in the room.

I can smell him.

Coffee, whiskey, icing sugar.

A sense of calm overwhelms me.

He unzips my wedding dress from behind, pulls me close, and nuzzles his face into the back of my neck.

"Ebedi öpücük," Ibrahim whispers.

He brushes hair away from my skin and slowly licks my neck along the vertebrae. He slips a knife into my hand. The handle is steel—cold in my palm. My fingers wrap around the handle as if it was made especially for my grip. My breath slows, thickens with want, so much so I can hear my blood pulse through my head.

"Do it," Ibrahim says.

Without a moment's hesitation I slice through Kimiko's jugular and admire the magnitude of the blood's flow.

I have returned home.

I am free.

I am once again—me.

chapter 55

mia
blood on my tongue

The road is cold and rough against my left cheek—the white reflection of the moon ripples in the pool of blood between me and Dad.

I blink, wince at a sharp pain in my thigh. I touch it with my right hand. It's wet, warm—a moist memory.

"Dad?" I whisper.

His eyelids flutter.

"Nash." I whisper a little louder, hoping he'll respond to his name instead. He remains still, silent, skeletal. I try to reach for him, but my left arm won't move. I'm not sure if I can even feel it.

Behind me, slow movement shifts the air. Someone curses under their breath and kicks a rock. It tumbles, rolls to a halt in the distance.

Gentle footsteps approach from behind. Someone sniffs, groans, and clears their throat; another voice whimpers.

A switchblade flicks open. The sound hovers in the air.

A small gasp. Female.

"What happened? What's going on?"

A man coughs, spits on the road—it splatters like phlegm. He tells the woman to shut the fuck up.

"Oh my God, I can't feel my legs. I can't feel my legs!" she cries.

"Don't move, ya cunt—stay in the fuckin' car." The man's voice quivers, his tone anxious, familiar. I think I know who it is. But it can't be. He wouldn't do something like this.

He loves me.

I roll onto my side, clenching my teeth through the sharp stabbing in my leg, and look towards the voices.

It's Mum, her face covered in blood, trapped in a mutilated rent-a-car wrapped around a tree. What is she doing here? Why?

My breath quickens. I look at the car, and at Dad, still motionless. Shooting pain crawls up my left arm and into my neck like an electric shock.

Did Mum run us over?

It is him. It's Mick.

And he has a knife to Mum's throat?

"Mick, no." I try to call out, but my voice is weak. My thigh feels like it's becoming one with the road, pounding I-told-you-sos via the stabbing sensations that keep spasming from my knee up to my breasts.

I should never have gotten involved in this.

"Mick!" I try again.

He turns his head.

"What are you doing? Leave her alone." I croak. "Help me. I don't think I can move."

Mick's eyes dart left to right; his Adam's apple moves up

and down, the whites of his eyes glowing under the street-lights.

"Are you okay, babe? Did you get hit hard?" Mick stutters, keeping the knife to Mum's throat. She whimpers like a child.

"I think so." The sentence comes out all shaky.

Mick nods and groans.

But I really don't know if I'm okay. I can't even tell how bad my injury is. All I know is that it hurts like hell.

"You shouldn't be here, babe," I say. "You were supposed to leave when Kimi got here."

"I wanted the cunt for myself. Did he come? Is he inside?"

"I dunno. I didn't see. Babe, Dad and I need help."

Mick's jaw tightens, and he flicks his chin towards Dad.

"He alive?"

An involuntary cry escapes my mouth. I've been trying to stay strong. But I can't. What if Dad's dead? I couldn't live with myself. How will I be able to forgive myself for not telling him about everything that very same day I got involved? I'm so fucking stupid.

"He's not moving." I wail.

"Fuck!" Mick kicks the side of Mum's car. She moans. "Where the fuck are the narcs?"

"What?" Mum gasps, seeming to have just come to. "Mia? What's going on?"

"Who the fuck is this cunt? You know 'er?" Mick snaps.

I nod, wincing in pain as I try to tell him who she is. I need a hospital. Why won't Mick just call an ambulance? "It's—my—my—mother."

"Shit!" Mick quickly pulls the knife away from Mum's throat and jumps back a few feet. He stares at her, then looks back at me.

"She a threat?"

"No."

Silence.

"Mick? Is that your name, little boy?" Mum's voice is high but slurred.

Mick curses under his breath. "The narcs should've been here by now. Fuck!"

"Mick, look at me," Mum says. Her voice sounds weak. Apologetic. "I need a hospital. So do Mia and Nash. Can you please call an ambulance for us? Whatever illegal stuff is going on, I won't say anything. Cross my heart and hope to die."

Mick paces for a bit, then kneels down beside me. He strokes my forehead, my cheek. His skin is warm and comforting against my cold goose-pimpled skin.

"Your leg's all fucked up, babe," he whispers.

I start to cry. "My arm feels weird too."

"Fuckin' hell. How fast was your mother drivin'?"

"I dunno, I . . . Oh fuck, fuck, fuck, Mick, my—my—my leg, it hurts!"

Mick stands and brings his hands to his head, breathing in and out so hard and fast that it makes me breathe faster too.

I'm going to die. I can feel it.

"Babe, we just have to tell the cops the truth," I whisper.

"We haven't done anything wrong. We haven't. Please, just call an ambulance. Please."

Mick paces, backwards and forwards, within the space of about two metres, his fingers to his mouth, biting off bits of nail and spitting them to the ground.

"But what about Mum 'n' Kimi? They're inside with a fuckin' shitload of drugs. They'll go to fuckin' prison. Something fucked up, I know it. I should bust in. Then I'll call an ambulance. I'll take the blame for everythin'. There's no other way."

"Babe, no! What if he's in there?" I feel like I'm shouting, but it sounds more like hot air with syllables.

"Your stupid fucking mother!" Mick yells. "What the fuck is she doin' here anyway?" He kicks the edge of the footpath multiple times.

"I'm sorry!" Mum cries. "I was—I think I must have passed out at the wheel. I don't know how this happened. It was an accident. But we all really need a hospital, Mick. I don't know what's—"

"Shh!" Mick jerks his head towards his house. There's a sound of a struggle coming from inside, and two evenly spaced gunshots fired.

Oh my God. It can't be. This can't be happening.

My heart slows, beats lazily in my ears, and I suddenly feel cold, weak, and breathless, the taste of blood on my tongue like live copper wire.

Then everything . . .

. . . starts to fade.

chapter 56

mick
i can taste it

I scream, "Fuck!" shaking Mia to stop 'er from closin' 'er eyes. "You need to stay awake, babe. Open ya eyes. Look at me. For fuck's sake, please."

Mia groans 'n' nods slowly, wincing 'n' reaching for her leg. "I'm tired. Just let me sleep."

I stroke her hair 'n' hold me breath. I'm not gonna be a fuckin' pussy. I'm gonna keep her alive. She *will* stay alive. "You're in shock, babe. You *need* to stay awake." I lean down 'n' kiss her on her forehead. I can't fuckin' believe this. I did this to 'er. I shouldn't've let her fuckin' get involved.

I whack meself on the head over 'n' over, repeatin' "fuck" over 'n' over.

Fuck what the cops think happened. Fuck me dad. There is always a next time. Always another fuckin' life. I jus' gotta take the rap. It's the only fuckin' way I can save Mia from this.

As I stand, Mia reaches out for me 'n' whimpers. "I love you," she says. I jus' wanna break down 'n' cry. But I can't. I gotta be strong. I gotta show Mia I have what it takes to look after 'er.

I take 'er hand 'n' close me eyes. "I'll call an ambulance,

babe. Really soon. Help will be here really fuckin' soon. Ya just gotta stay awake a little longer, babe. Promise me. I need to think a minute." I stroke 'er head. She's shakin' 'n' shit. I take me T-shirt off 'n' wrap it around the gash in her leg. I've seen people do that shit on TV. You know, to stop the bleedin' 'n' shit.

Mia's mum starts screamin' 'n' bangin' 'er hand into the jammed car door. She's never gonna get herself out like that. What the fuck does she think she's tryin' to pull? And she's gonna draw attention to us. We need to keep the cops away for as long as fuckin' possible. The neighbours have prob'ly already called someone about the car crash.

She screams again. It's so fuckin' ear-piercin' that a few people's porch lights turn on. If the neighbours come out of their houses now we're all totally screwed.

"Shut the fuck up," I hiss. "You wanna go to fuckin' prison?"

"You're the asshole that's going to prison! Get me outta this car!" Mia's mum growls like a psycho.

"Shh!" I spit. I've gotta find a fuckin' way to shut the bitch up.

"Get me out, get me out, get me out!" she screams.

Fuckin' great. We're doomed. A neighbour from across the street comes out onta their front lawn 'n' tells us to keep it down. He holds a hand up to his eyes. But then the look on his face changes, and he bolts to his front door, screaming for his wife to call the cops.

"Look what you've fucking done, you fucked up fuckin'

cunt!" I don't care if she's Mia's mum. Doesn't fuckin' matter now anyway. Everyone's starin' out their fuckin' windas.

I step closer to the car wreck and kick the door. "Are you fuckin' happy, bitch? Ya just sent ya daughter to prison for being a fuckin', ya know, thing, to drug trafficking."

"You don't know who I am," she squeals. "I have power. I can run you into the ground before the cops do. Now, get me the fuck out of this car before I make your life a living hell!"

Mia's mum's voice rings in me ears like a high-pitched siren. It switches somethin' on inside me that I've never felt before in me life. I pull me knife outta me back pocket, 'n' before I can even think to stop meself, I slit 'er fuckin' throat.

Everythin' goes quiet. All I can 'ear is me heart thumpin' in me ears. The thrill of the cut pulsin' through me body like petrol.

But then it hits me what I've done. And I throw up.

I just fuckin' murdered someone. The *mother* of the girl I love.

What the fuck did I just do . . . ?

I turn to face me house 'n' see the side door fling open.

And two shadowy figures drag two bodies inta the back-yard.

Mum? No, no, *no*, not me mum!

chapter 57

sonia
ebedi öpücük

Ibrahim wraps Kimi and his fleuro-green-capped side-kick in the black garden plastic. He secures it with rope, grunting as he ties the last knot around Kimi's neck.

He pulls the bag of fertilizer out of the shed. It pelts down with rain. My hair and dress quickly become cold and wet.

I shiver, staring at Ibrahim, trying to remain as still as possible, not to show emotion. It's how he likes it—corpse bride. I wonder if we are going to get away with this, why he killed his sidekick. Is this part of some grand scheme to get me back on his side? Was threatening Mick a way to get closer to me, knowing very well that I'd do anything to protect our son from living his parents' fate? Did he send Kimiko to tempt Mia with drugs to get to us through Nash?

Ibrahim smiles.

Steps closer.

Slow. Steady.

His footsteps silent amidst the slick splashing of rain on the plastic-covered bodies.

Ibrahim cups my face in his hands. Water drips from his nose. He kisses me—I breath in—our wet mouths blending together like dough.

Gentle.

Soft.

I'm his "forever kiss."

"Ebedi öpücük." Ibrahim sighs. "Run away with me."

I tremble and nod, but hold still as Ibrahim uses one hand to massage my breast. He moves his hand down my stomach, lifts my dress, and his fingers crawl inside the front of my pants. He runs a finger gently over my clitoris. I shiver and close my eyes.

His breath is sweet.

Turkish Delight.

Tempting. Delicious. Dangerous. I open my eyes again.

He smirks.

I refuse to react.

Until he cups a hand over my mouth and shoves his fingers inside me. I let out a deep moan.

"You're mine," he says.

Yes. Yes, I am.

chapter 58

mick

astagh firol lahal-lathi la ...

I dart across me fuckin' nature strip. Duck behind a bush by me front fence to try 'n' get closer. To see what the fuck's goin' on, but it's too fuckin' dark, too dark to see, fuck!

Shit shit shit, you stupid mother fuck dick.

My breathing becomes heavy 'n' quick 'n' shit. I yank me phone from me back pocket 'n' almost flick it over the fence. I catch it midair 'n' dial. Me hand is shakin'; I'm hummin' the notes the zero makes as I press it three times.

It rings 'n' rings. Aren't emergency services s'posed to pick up fast, for fuck's sake? It's freezing tonight, 'n' me fingertips feel like they're going to snap off.

Come on come on come on come on . . . pick up, ya fuckheads!

"Police, Fire, or Ambulance?"

I hammer the front of me forehead with one finger.

"Police, Fire, or Ambulance, sir?"

"Ambulance. Fuck!"

"Location?"

"What?"

"Your address or whereabouts, sir."

"88 Grandfield Drive, Thornbury." I look above the bush

to check if Mia or Nash are movin', but they're not, 'n' in me chest, me chest, it's heavy 'n' tight 'n' feels like I can't breathe, 'n' tears start comin' outta me eyes 'n' down me cheeks 'n' inta the corner of me mouth. And the back of me throat feels like me father is chokin' me—he *is* choking me, with his mind, his existence—me fuckin' dad is ruinin' the only fuckin' chance I have ever had at true love.

The phone blips 'n' sounds like it's being put through to someone else.

"Hello, an ambulance is on its way to 88 Grandfield Drive, Thornbury. Please confirm that this is the correct location."

"Yes!" I hiss. "It'll come quick, right? It won't take long?"

"No, sir. Please state your—"

I let the phone slip from me hand 'n' crash to the ground as I stand up. I stare at Mia, passed out on the road, 'n' choke on the thought of me mother wrapped up in garbage bags buried in the backyard. I bring me hands to me throat thinkin' I still got me T-shirt on. It feels like the collar is chokin' me.

It's all me. I can't blame me dad for this. I did this meself. I put Mia's life in danger. I'm never gonna fuckin' forgive meself.

It's me last fuckin' chance to do something right for 'er.

The only way Mia is gonna be okay—the only way she'll ever be happy—is if she has nothin' at all to do with me again.

I run indoors 'n' grab me mum's pistol from the table by the front door.

I stand in the doorway, where the rug is, drop to me knees, 'n' shut me eyes—hard—so hard that me vision turns white, like light from Allah is gracin' me. I can pretend he's gracin' me.

I pray, quietly, quickly, quietly, for the first time in fuckin' ages, for Allah to forgive me sins: *Astagh firol lahal-lathi la ilaha illa howal hayyal qayyoma w'atooba ilayh. Astagh firol lahal-lathi la ilaha illa howal hayyal qayyoma w'atooba ilayh. Astagh firol lahal-lathi la ilaha illa howal hayyal qayyoma w'atooba ilayh.*

Then I hold the pistol to me head.

chapter 59

sonia

$$v = d/t$$

A gunshot fires from inside the house. I gasp, sucking Ibrahim's palm to my mouth—his sweat, my saliva, our flesh, the magnetic rush of his forbidden touch thrilling me into submission.

Ibrahim pulls back as though I gave him an electric shock. He squints at me, shakes his head. His sharp wet jaw glistens in the moonlight.

Our heavy breathing slips into sync.

"What if it's Mick?" I whisper, or maybe only mouth—maybe only think.

Ibrahim nods—a curt flick of his head in the direction of the house.

I bolt to the back door, through the kitchen, and down the hall, my breath pulsing in and out of my chest—faster, heavier, hotter.

I reach the entrance of the hallway, and my breathing stops, my heartbeat pounding in my ears.

Mick's lying in a pool of blood near the front door.

For a moment—a very short moment—

Time.

Stops.

***

"Mick!" I scream, gasping for air, over and over—a fish out of water. "Oh my God, Mick, no, no, no—" My veins pulsate in my throat as I rush to his side. I try to swallow, I can't, I'm choking, choking on my own tears and regret and years upon years of neglect.

I wrap my arms around him, cradle him, crying his name over and over, the scent of his blood a sting in my nose. I stroke his forehead, crying, smearing his blood all over his face, my hands.

I stop.

My pistol rests in his limp fingers.

I pick it up. Stare at it in my shaking hand.

It's my fault. It's *all* my fault.

I killed my only son. I *murdered* my son!

Sirens. Sirens. Sirens grow louder, shrilling, pounding, louder, breathing, crying, screaming, screeching through me, pulsing, pushing, pounding in my head.

Flashing lights and police commands encompass the space around me. Heavy footsteps, running, yelling, suck the air from the room, and I try to cry mercy but I can't, I can't, I can't breathe.

The commotion comes to a complete halt when I look up at them, their guns, their weapons, their anger—fear and fulfillment reflect from their faces.

I drop the gun and lift my blood-smeared hands above my head. Three officers stand at the open front door shining torches straight into my eyes, aiming guns at my heart.

This is it.

This is how it ends.

chapter 60

mia
seven months later

I sit in front of the glass, waiting for Sonia to be escorted out of her cell. It's been weeks since I've been to visit as I've spent the last few months talking to a lawyer about how to get Sonia out of prison. But he's convinced her testimony will not hold up in court without Dad and Mick as witnesses.

And of course, with Ibrahim nowhere to be found, there isn't any proof that he was even the slightest bit involved. The only fingerprints on the gun Mick shot himself with were his own and Sonia's. And Ibrahim somehow got rid of the bodies of Kimi and his sidekick without a trace. Their Missing Persons reports are just that—missing persons' reports. So there isn't even any proof that they are dead.

And my mum. My fucked-up mum. I don't think I will ever understand what went on there. What was she doing following us? Why was she driving so fast? The cops said that she was doped up on sedatives, but that she had some kind of paradoxical reaction to them.

I don't get it.

That doesn't explain why she was *there*.

Sometimes I wonder whether Dad knew. And I think

back to that weird phone conversation, and the follow-up dinner in that weird purple restaurant. Did he really just want to ask me about Sonia then? Or was it actually about my mum? Maybe I'm looking too deeply into it. I hope so. I'm not sure how I'd feel about Dad keeping that from me. And I wouldn't really be able to do anything about it now anyway.

And Mick.

I don't think I'll ever understand why he did what he did. Well, maybe I do. Maybe he did it to protect me and Dad. Or maybe he did it simply to escape arrest. I hope—every day—that it's the former.

Dad and I sat staring at Mick in his hospital bed for hours. Still in a coma. On life support. But I felt like he could hear me. Like he was still looking out for us. I need to remember him in a good way, in case he wakes up. If it wasn't for my mum being at the wrong place at the wrong time, would any of this have happened? Or what about if I hadn't taken the drugs from Kimi?

Or is the taste for crime really in the blood forever, and it wouldn't have made a difference at all?

Maybe.

Maybe it's a curse.

But Mick is so much more than what he seems. He's smart. And I love him.

I guess, in the end, that's all that matters.

Love. I will love him even if he doesn't ever wake up.

A buzzer rings, and Sonia walks through a heavy metal

door, hands cuffed in front of her. What the hell for? She's not a murderer. She's not a criminal. Whatever happened to being innocent until proven guilty? I can't believe they are putting her through this. All she was trying to do was protect her family.

Plain and simple.

Why won't anyone believe her? It was all Ibrahim.

"Any progress?" Sonia's voice is raspy, and she has a big black bruise on her left cheek the size of an apricot.

I shake my head. "Not until we can locate Ibrahim. It's impossible. The case against you is solid without him or the bodies. Are you sure you have *no* idea where he is?"

Sonia nods, coughs, and clutches at her side in pain.

"Are you alright?" I ask.

Sonia smiles wryly. "What do you think?"

I don't know what to say. I just stare at her.

"How's your arm and leg? Better?"

I nod. "Much. The scars are starting to fade a bit."

"That's good." Sonia smiles at me with apologetic warmth. I really don't understand how she can manage anything but self-pity right now. I guess she has always been a good person deep down. It was Ibrahim that tainted her. I'm sure of it.

I swallow a buildup of saliva. "I've gotta go. I had to bring Dad with me today, and he's waiting outside."

"Nash? He is here? Why didn't you bring him in? I would have loved to see him."

"They wouldn't let me."

"Why not?"

"Not sure. Something to do with him not being lucid. He's come in here before. I don't get what the problem is."

Sonia shrugs. "You didn't question it?"

"I didn't have the strength to argue."

Sonia coughs again. "Okay, well—I'll try to sort it out for next time." She looks down; the smile on her face remains. She is trying so hard to be normal around me. I really look up to her for that. I wouldn't be so strong in her situation.

"I guess I'll be in touch," I say, and flatten both hands on the glass—the closest I can get them to her. Sonia does the same, directly on mine, like we are taking each other's handprints off the glass. We hold each other's gaze for a moment more and share a few silent words of hope.

When we lower our hands, I stand and say, "I wrote a rock version of 'Somewhere Over the Rainbow' for you."

It looks as though Sonia's breath catches in her throat. "You remember my rainbow story?"

I nod. "Of course I do. It's the only thing that keeps me going. I'll play it for you when you get out."

A tear falls down Sonia's cheek as I step away from the glass.

***

Dad is staring into space when I approach him in the waiting room. He's sitting on a bench, peeling the banana he shoved in his pocket on the way out of the house.

I kneel in front of him and rest my hands on his thighs. "Do you want to go get some lunch? Pizza and beer?"

Dad nods. "Mia? That's your name, isn't it?"

I squeeze Dad's knees. "Yes, that's my name."

Dad rests his half-peeled banana in his lap and touches a hand to my cheek. It's cold and clammy. He looks into my eyes as if he suddenly remembers who I am, but his eyes glaze over again just as fast.

He lowers his hand and scrutinizes his surroundings. "Where are we?"

"It's not important," I say. "What's important is that I'm about to take you out for a real yummy pizza. You're hungry, right?"

Dad looks at the banana in his lap as if it were a weapon. I pick it up and hold it in front of him. "Would you still like to eat this?"

"Did I want to eat it before?"

"I think so. You were peeling it when I came out."

"Came out of where?" Confusion spreads across his face and his bottom lip trembles. "I'm sorry. I'm being forgetful today. What's your name again?"

I stand from my crouching position and sit beside him on the bench. I take his hand and pat it gently. He looks puzzled but not at all afraid. He has always been good at hiding that.

This is my dad now. The longest he remembers who I am is five minutes, usually less. A tear tickles my cheek, and I wipe it away with the heel of my hand.

"My name is Mia, Nash." I try not to call him Dad because that always triggers more confused questions.

Dad smiles and squeezes the tops of my still-quite-flabby arms.

"Well, Mia," Dad says, then runs his thumb under my right eye as if removing some smudged mascara. "You are the most beautiful woman I have ever met."

epilogue

sonia

$$F_n = \sum_{k=0}^{\left[\frac{n-1}{2}\right]} \binom{n-k-1}{k}$$

It's one past midnight. In the corridor.

I lean my back against the wall next to the phone box. I have permission to make one call today.

Just one.

I only need one. One is the beginning of everything. The first step beyond zero. As soon as you step forward and take advantage of one, the spiral begins and never ends. It's written in the sequence.

I close my eyes and hold my breath for a moment, but long enough to hear the shuffle of inmates' feet echo in rhythm with my heart. The heart that beats for the love of my life.

A man so cruel, but so kind.

Deep down. He's kind. Deep down. He loves me.

We are a team.

No matter how much I pretended to regret that life, for the sake of my son, I couldn't help but keep going back. Of course, I should have known. It's written in the sequence.

All these years, I've tried to hide from myself. Tried to hide inside the numbers. Each equation a sedative, a code for escape.

Every day I write a new number from the sequence in my little notebook. I found it under my bed when I arrived. It was meant for me. Because on the cover is a zero. A fresh number each day. It's all I need . . . 1, 1, 2, 3, 5, 8, 13, 21, 34, 55, 89, 144, 233, 377, 610, 987, 1597, 2584, 4181, 6765 . . .

The only other numbers I see are the ones printed on prisoners' backs. So I play a little game with myself. I've been adding them up every twenty-four hours for the last seven months. And if they match the numbers I've written in my book, I call him. Because Ibrahim is my number one. And I am his. And no matter what happens, we will always exist side by side. It's written in the sequence.

The number one is also known as "unity": the probability of an event that is almost certain to occur; the first figurate number of every kind. It is neither a prime number nor a composite number but completely unique. It's the atomic number of hydrogen and the ultimate reality and source of all existence. See where I'm going with this?

We're written in the sequence.

My hands shake as I dial Ibrahim's untraceable number; the tone of the old 80's phone mimicking the purr of the voice I'm about to hear on the other end.

"Hello?"

"Baby?" My heart steadies.

"Ebedi öpücük. I knew you'd come to your senses."

"Ibrahim. You've got to get me out of here. I've got the most brilliant plan."

Ibrahim laughs. Deep, gentle. "You do?"

I smile, look left to right to make sure no one is in earshot. If they're monitoring this call, they'll be out to stop it at any second because Ibrahim's number is untraceable. So I need to be quick.

I rest my right hand over my left breast, like I'm about to take a pledge, and whisper, "You're going to be so proud of me. He's in. He's finally in. After *all* these years. He's our number two."

"How do you know?"

"Because he's still pretending, like we asked. He loves me. He's protecting you. For me."

Silence.

"Can we trust him?"

"Of course. Nash is loyal when it comes to love. And Mia doesn't suspect a thing."

acknowledgements

Once again there are many individuals—writers, editors, friends and family—I'd like to thank for helping me in various degrees during the creation of this book.

First and foremost I'd like to thank my partner, Spilios Tzemos, for being a loving "husband" (We're not married, but I like to call him that. We do have an eight-year-old mortgage and a seven-year-old dog, so that pretty much counts as marriage, don't you think?) and for putting up with the endless hours I spend at the computer.

Many thanks go to my parents, Erika Bach and Demetri Vlass, for encouraging me to reach for my dreams and never give up ever since I was a little girl.

Huge thanks to my beta readers, Matthew MacNish, Dawn Ius, and Trisha Farnan. If it wasn't for you I wouldn't have even known that Sonia was really a killer.

Thank you to Francine Howarth for choosing the name Kimiko (it was originally Summer).

Thank you Anthony Bell (my other Dad) and Dan Holloway for the mathematics advice. I honestly had no clue, and I really wanted the equations to be symbolic. I couldn't have done that without you both.

Thanks to my uncle, Jim Baum, for making sure the crime stuff—although very little—was authentic (as a writer there are great benefits to having a cop in the family), and to my editors Susanne Lakin and Amie McCracken for making sure those gate-crashing typos didn't hang around for the big party.

Thank you Adam Byatt for making me laugh when I asked my friends on Facebook, "What material would a wedding dress need to be made of in order to make a swishing sound when the woman walks?" by replying with, "Her dress swished like a pair of corduroy trousers and generated enough static electricity to power a small household appliance. She dare not risk touching the cat for fear of transferring the power and exploding the cat into bite size nibbles."

Thanks to Erika Olsen and Peggy Wheeler for confirming that taffeta would in fact *swish*. I decided not to mention the material of Sonia's wedding dress, but that's beside the point.

And of course, a very special thanks to Amie McCracken for her enormous help in producing *The Bell Collection* edition.

And thank YOU for reading!

Enjoyed this book?
Go to *vineleavespress.com/books*
to find more from *The Bell Collection*.

To sign up to Jessica's newsletter and/or connect with her on social media go to *jessicabellauthor.com/contact*.

Are you a writer?
You might be interested in Jessica's
Writing in a Nutshell series.